Copyright©2015 by Christopher Woods

Cover art by Derrick Gallagher

Books by Christopher woods
<u>Soulguard Series</u>
Soulguard
Soullord
Bloodlord
Rash'Tor'Ri (forthcoming)

<u>This Fallen World Novellas</u>
This Fallen World
Broken City
Power Play (forthcoming)

Acknowledgements:

Once again, I would like to thank all of you who have bought my books and made all of this possible. As always, I would like to thank my wife, Wendy Woods for all of her love and support.

Bloodlord
Soulguard: Book 3
Christopher Woods

Prologue

Beliniea rounded the corner as she heard Joran's voice.

"The Prophet is coming!" the boy yelled, "He will speak in the square."

Bel grabbed the boy's arm as he was running by, "Did you say the Prophet? He is a myth. No one can stand up to them. They're killed on sight."

"No, Bel," the boy said earnestly, "Pitre saw him at Kel'Doran."

"Pitre is a crazy old man, boy," she said with narrowed eyes. "You're going to get in trouble of you keep this up."

He pulled from her grasp, "I'm not lying Bel! He's almost here. You just wait and see! He's real!"

The boy turned and ran down the street yelling his news at the top of his lungs. Bel shook her head sadly. He would be in front of her father before the day was out. Guserd wouldn't...couldn't let this boy draw the attention of their Kresh masters. They would slaughter whole villages without any sort of warning.

Could it be true, though? Was there a man who stood and killed Kresh? She knew they could die. She had seen it three cycles ago when the Kresh'Far fell from the Escarpment. It fell so far. When she had found it, it was squirming around. All of its bones had been broken and it was in an immense amount of pain.

"Kill me," it had uttered, almost too quiet to hear. But Bel had heard it. When she shoved her dagger into its left eye into its brain she saw the life leave its other eye. They can die.

But it had lived through such a fall. How could one man defeat such as that? The Prophet had to be a myth.

She heard the ruckus at the far end of the street and turned to find herself looking at a man striding down the street toward her. He wore a flowing black robe that barely cleared the ground.

Bel saw his right hand as he strode by. It had scars along the back of it, burn scars. She couldn't tell how far they reached up his arm. The robe covered too much.

Bel stepped forward and joined the growing crowd of people following him down the street.

"Prophet..."

"Killed hundreds..."

She grimaced as she heard the comments. He probably had done something like she had and made it all into some grand story.

He stopped in the center of the square and turned to the crowd of people following him.

"Good day, friends," His voice was deep but Bel couldn't take her eyes from his face. His eyes were so vibrant, like they barely contained all of the life within them. They seemed to burn with a fire from the inside.

"I come to you today to tell you about what is coming." His voice carried to all corners of the square, yet he didn't yell.

"Freedom approaches," he said. "That is not a word many here know anything about. Freedom has been taken from you long before any of you were even born. But I tell you, here today, you will see it again. Within your lifetime, you will see that freedom."

"Mister," Bel cringed as she heard her father's voice, "you endanger this whole community to spout this nonsense. We can't allow you to continue. I've heard this term, Freedom. I hear it from the ones taken from the Doran Colony. But they all find that it is an illusion. Even they are not free. The Kresh mass to extinguish that colony as we speak."

"They will try," the Prophet returned, "They face something they have never seen before when they try to destroy Doran colony. You have heard rumors of Rash'Tor'Ri? Of life Ender?"

"Scary stories told to Kresh children!"

The Prophet's laughter rolled across the square.

"Life Ender is not a fable, nor a Myth. He is not a God, nor is he a Devil. He is a man. Yet he is a man unlike any man you have ever seen. Six Lunar cycles back, the Kresh sent a force to that colony. There is a man among you who witnessed that event. His name is Pitre, I believe."

Bel watched old Pitre stand up. Her eyes widened as the Prophet smiled, and motioned for Pitre to come forth.

"Will you kindly tell them what you saw, Elder?"

"I will, Prophet," Pitre said. "I saw so many Kresh they covered the whole plain. There were Kresh'Far, Kresh'Sor'An, Kresh'Ma'Nar, and even a Kresh'Farrara'Ti. They passed through the gate to Doran."

"Then what did you see?" the Prophet asked softly.

"They continued through the Gate for a long time until there was a great burst of some hellish fire from the gate, and in a few moments, Kresh'Sor'An came back through the gate."

"And how many of them were there?"

Pitre hung his head, "I can only count to ten, Prophet. But I counted to ten four times and then to five once."

The Prophet glanced across the crowd.

"There are about twice that amount standing here today. And Pitre, what sort of shape were these forty five Kresh'Sor'An?"

"They were burned, badly, Prophet. And they were afraid."

"They were afraid!" the Prophet's voice boomed. "Do you know what they were afraid of? I do. On the other side of that gate stood Life Ender. And when he has stopped the Kresh from coming for his world, he will come here. He will come to set this world free!"

Bel was mesmerized by the Prophet. There were no more attempts to stop him from speaking. It seemed that he had mesmerized the whole village.

"And so we are back to that word you really do not understand. Freedom. Freedom is the right to choose your own destiny. The right to live without the fear of being killed out of hand because you don't agree with your masters. Freedom means, no one is another's master. This is what freedom is, my friends."

The Prophet stopped, and raised his fiery eyes toward the horizon. They narrowed as he saw or sensed something.

"They are coming," he said.

He stepped forward, and the crowd parted in front of him. He walked up the street toward the north.

"Hide as best you can, friends," he said, "Kresh are coming."

The words registered on the crowd, and there was pandemonium. The villagers scrambled for their homes or anywhere they could hide. Wails filled the air for they knew what it meant when Kresh came to the villages. Slaughter would follow.

Beliniea drew the dagger from its hidden sheath. She would not die fleeing the Masters. She would fight to her last breath. She wished that the rumors of the Prophet could have been true. But now all that was left was to die with pride. She looked to her left to find her father standing with a similar blade in his hand. Along with them stood seven others of the villagers, all of which Bel knew well.

The Kresh came over the horizon and Bel saw that there were hundreds of them. She held back the fear and tears that she wanted to let loose. She would die as a woman, not a sniveling child.

"Freedom," boomed the voice of the Prophet as he strode toward the Kresh, "Freedom is not cheap. It is paid for in blood! Our blood or theirs!"

She saw his hands unclasp the robe at his neck. A thrill ran through her at the utter bravery of this man. He wasn't like any other she had ever met. He could have run the other direction. He had no family here, no one that he must protect. Yet he strode toward the horde of Kresh'Far that neared the edge of the village. Could the rumors really be true?

"Today!" his voice boomed as he flung his arms wide and the robe flipped backward and rippled toward the ground.

Bel could see the burns along his right side and over his arms. His trousers covered his lower body, but she could see the burns extending to his waistline and knew they went further.

She gasped as flames seemed to spring from within the Prophet, and flow across his body.

"Today, that price will be paid in their blood!" he roared, and grasped the hilts of a pair of blades strapped in crossing sheaths on his back.

He drew these blades that sprang to fiery life, and launched himself toward the Kresh. He moved so fast, she could hardly see him. Then she felt something jar her insides. Her teeth hurt, and her brain seemed to vibrate.

THRUUMMM!

Fire exploded in front of the Prophet, and it seemed as if the world would burn away in front of him. Kresh were incinerated. Ashes filled the sky, and she heard something that sent a great surge of satisfaction through her whole being.

She heard the screams of terror from those that had terrorized her people as long as she could remember.

Chapter 1

I awoke abruptly. I'd been dreaming, but I couldn't remember exactly what it had been. Sometimes it's like that. Sometimes my dreams are so vivid, they plague me, and other times they just fade away.

I looked to my left to see my angel lying peacefully beside me, a curl of her hair dangling across her forehead. I almost feel human when I'm with Lyrica. She doesn't have the fear I see in almost every other person with which I deal.

She always tells me that I see fear because that's what I look for in people. I can't help that it's what my eye perceives first.

"She could be right," I muttered as I eased out of the bed.

I walked quietly to the window, and looked outside at the garden growing outside our house in Oklahoma. The Romanians I had marked, when we had taken the Shak'Tar base, had built this for us to stay in whenever we could get away.

The garden looked so peaceful, and it was hard to believe we had just been in a huge battle earlier this year. The Kresh had been distressingly quiet for six months. I knew they were still there, as my new Soulstream would fluctuate when the gates opened periodically. But there were no attacks from them as of yet.

I saw several children run through the yard of the next house. They stopped and waved at me, and continued on their way. It was a little disconcerting, because they couldn't physically see me, but knew exactly where I was. I can't help but feel guilty for the Mark that I had forced on these people.

Lyrica stirred behind me and I turned to her, I saw beautiful green eyes and a smile.

"Mornin', Beautiful", I said with a smile.

"Morning, my love," she answered.

It sends a chill through me when she says that to me. She is my Soulmate, my other half, the better half I'm certain.

"What say we go join the others for breakfast?" I suggested.

"It figures," she muttered, "always hungry."

"I'm not always hungry," I said, "just when I'm awake."

Meals were a grand thing to the Romanians. They would all come together and eat. There would be enormous amounts of food, and everyone would be there. My escorts tend to love it when we come here. It's probably some of the best food that can be had, and they are treated like old friends by all who live at the Farm.

It bothers me a little that they treat me and Lyrica as royalty. But there's nothing I can do about that. They'd be offended if I ordered them not to.

They're in better shape, by far, than they would have been as slaves of the Kresh where I had found them. Or even worse, used as fodder for the Kresh armies.

"I'm pretty sure you're hungry in your sleep too," she answered, "Let's go put something in your bottomless pit."

"I hope they made that sausage they had yesterday," I said, "and the skinny pancakes."

"Crepes," she said.

"Those were awesome."

This was bound to be much more fun than the meeting I was scheduled to have with Paige, later on. I was going to have to bring up a subject that might be considered a problem to the Soulguard. It was too late to do anything about it. I'd already set everything in motion, and it would happen regardless of the approval of the Archmage and Council.

But, for now, I would just enjoy a meal with my "family".

***

"Hello, Colin," Paige said as I walked into her office, "How is Lyrica? And your Romanians, how are they?"

"Lyrica is fine, and the Romanians have made the Farm completely self-sufficient. They even have a pretty good profit margin. They keep it in trust for me, although, I tried to give it all to them. So it just keeps growing. Maybe it can carry them through if we have some bad years."

"That's good," she said, "Gregor should be here in a moment. Then you can tell me what you've been so tight lipped about."

Gregor entered the office, and sat down beside me.

"Colin," he said with a nod, "How are you?"

"I'm good," I said. "How are the politicians treatin' ya?"

"Every now and then they get rambunctious, but they straighten up when I tell them you're going to have to come deal with things if we can't settle our differences."

I heard a snort and a chuckle from the other side of the desk.

"They're just afraid he'll blow something up," Paige said.

"I have no idea what you're talkin' about," I said.

"Sure you don't," She said, "Now, tell me what it is that you didn't want to say over a phone."

"OK, here goes. Four months ago Warren acquired a company for me that specialized in programming. They were tasked with creating a system that we can use to mimic the brain that it's connected to. They've succeeded. I've put into motion the building of a weapon that uses this system. I'm at the stage where I need to put some Mages in the building of these weapons, which would need the approval of the Archmage."

"And just what do you need Mages for in the building of these weapons?" Paige asked with eyes narrowed.

"Source weapons," Gregor answered before I could.

Paige let out a long slow breath. I could see she was angry without even looking at her aura.

"You didn't think this was something you should have run through the Council before building?"

"The Council may have said no," I answered.

"With good reason!" She returned, "Do you realize how dangerous it is to put that kind of power out there for just anyone to use?"

"Do you realize how dangerous it would be not to?" I answered with a little rage leaking through my mental walls. "I plan to arm the world. There are millions of Kresh over there, and they want us dead. We've been lucky so far, but how long will it last 'til they come through a gate we know nothing about? How many do you think they could get over here before we could mount any sort of defense?"

"You automatically assume the council would say no..."

"No I didn't," I answered, "but I didn't need the council behind this until I found out it would work."

Gregor had been quiet through most of this but when he spoke, it was right to the point.

"We need them."

Paige had opened her mouth to say something else to me, but stopped and looked at Gregor.

He continued, "I am one of the 'Old Guard' you might say. We've protected our secrets for a thousand years. It's hard to change that sort of thinking, but we must. This is a new war they are bringing to us. They'll keep draining our numbers until there are no Soulguard left to face them. The world needs weapons to use that are efficient and effective. We can't be everywhere, and with weapons like that the world can, possibly, defend itself."

Paige was quiet for a time, "The weapons don't bother me as much as someone not trusting us to make the right decision."

She looked at me with eyes narrowed.

"Paige, I'm bringing it to you right now."

This attitude was grating on me. I'd spent the majority of the fortune that Warren had built for me on this project.

"I needed something solid to bring to you, and I have it now. I'm here now because I do trust you to make the right decision about supporting the project. Frankly, I have no idea why you're so pissed off. When have I ever done anything like this without the welfare of our world at the top of my list of reasons why?"

"Because you hid it from me!"

She was hurt because she thought I didn't trust her. She had always been one of the few people I could trust to have my back, and she thought I didn't trust her any more.

"I wasn't hiding it," I said. "I haven't mentioned it to anyone. Anyone. Warren is the only person who fully knows what we are doing. I needed something that works before telling anyone about it. You and Gregor are now the third and fourth person to be brought into it. You have no reason to believe that I don't trust you. Now that I have a working prototype, I need to bring it out in the open. You were always the first person on my list of people to tell about the project."

I could see her anger subsiding, and knew she would be alright. She'd honestly thought I didn't trust her anymore. The job was weighing on her more and more. I could see how that would happen. Everything tends to be the fault of the one in charge. She was catching all the grief from every angle pertaining to the Soulguard, and there was a lot of it.

"So how about you let us see these weapons of yours?" Gregor suggested.

"I have to meet with Marco and Polo," I said, "Then we can get to that. I have to get them to let me get some volunteers to learn to use 'em."

"I can't believe you call two generals, Marco and Polo," Paige said.

"They actually liked the names, and started usin' them on each other. They even say it like the game when they see each other. 'Marco!' 'Polo!'. It's great."

She just shook her head.

Chapter 2

I sat in my office waiting on Seran Polomo and Marcus Stratton. Both of them were National Guard Generals, Polomo or "Polo" was Army National Guard, while Marcus or "Marco" was Air National Guard. Both of them were veterans, and both of them were my friends.

I was positive they would be thrilled to know about the new weapons, right up to the moment they found out I would be distributing them to every nation in the world. Then there might be a little friction. I didn't expect the friction from them, personally, but from the government when they found that they wouldn't be in control of the whole thing.

That's what had been our biggest struggle throughout the last six months since Second Kansas. Just another thing left for Paige and Gregor to deal with amongst the politicians.

I could see both of their souls as they neared the building. I could see Rostov out front with Prada. My Mage squad took turns partnering with Prada as my "bodyguards" after the loss of Rictor at Second Kansas.

I had left my door open so the two Generals walked on in.

"Good afternoon, Colin," Polo said with a smile, "I understand you have some good news for us today."

"Yep, very good news," I said. "What would you guys think about a weapon that is fed by the Source?"

"You've talked about making cannons out near the gate like that before." Marco said.

"Yeah but these are personal weapons for soldiers. They work a lot like the Soullance a Mage uses."

I saw Polomo's eyes widen at the thought of that along with a surge of excitement rolling through his aura.

"You have these?"

"I have a proto-type," I said, "I need some volunteers to learn how to use em. That's where you come in. I need some soldiers."

"We'll need to see the proto-type work before we can authorize tests with our troops," he said, "but I see no reason why you can't have the men afterwards."

"As soon as we see that, we can turn the engineers loose to start manufacturing..." Marcus said but stopped as he saw my wince.

You don't reach the rank these two had reached without being fairly sharp.

"We're not going to like the next part, are we?" Polomo asked.

"This whole thing has been privately funded," I said, "for a reason. These weapons will be available world-wide. I want the whole world armed, if I can get it."

"I can see where our bosses would be a little upset with that since the US is the only place that's been attacked thus far," Polomo stated. "But I see where you would want to do it this way. The Kresh aren't going to just hit here."

"They probably won't be comin' here when they come back," I said. "My spies tell me that they're settling who is next in line to take over the attack. When they do, they'll be back, and I think they'll come through somewhere we haven't seen yet. There are five gates unaccounted for. It's gonna be ugly."

"I just hope we have time to get the guns working and out there before they do come back. I would love to meet them with a wave of the Source weapons," I continued.

"Ok," Marcus nodded, "We'll worry with that part later. So, tell us about the weapons."

"They're based on the Soullance, as I said. The weapon itself is quite simple. It looks much like a big shotgun. Inside the barrels are focusing lenses to make the power more intense."

As I said this I pulled a folder from the top drawer of my desk. Inside were drawings of the weapon I was describing.

"The barrels are removable so they can be replaced. You can only do so much continuous fire before the barrel degrades."

"Interesting," Polo said.

"The key to the whole thing is the software developed by my programmers. It makes the link between the helmet and the gun work. With the helmet on, anyone can feel the Source through the weapon, and Pull it like a Mage. It will only Pull through the gun, instead of the person. Thus, no ammo needed. Heavy use will need barrels, though. We haven't found anything that can handle the heat that's generated by the Source for very long."

"Very impressive, Colin," Marcus said, "Where did the private funding come from, if I may ask? Soulguard?"

"Actually, I mean very privately funded," I answered, "by me. Over the years, my finance guy has made a lot of money for me. Almost all of it went into this project."

"What's the price tag on these weapons?"

"Bare minimum," I returned, "We'll be sellin' close to cost. Maybe a few percent above, so I can get my money back out of it."

"It sounds good, Colin. When can we see a test?"

"I'm plannin' a test for Paige and Gregor on Friday. You guys are more than welcome to come too. After you see it, I'm hoping to set up another one for you, and whoever you need to bring into it. There will be demonstrations for most of the foreign governments as well. I'm hopin' we can get into production within a month and start the training. My test guy says it's not hard to learn. He picked it up almost immediately."

"I'm looking forward to it," Polo said with a grin. "It's time we evened up the playing field with these bastards. We can face 'em even when your guys can't get there in time. The attacks here would have gone a totally different direction if we'd had these."

"New York, Chicago, Atlanta," Marco said with a shake of his head, "all would have been better. Not to mention LA, that was a catastrophe. Thank God for your boy, Graves."

"You're right there," I said. "I'm not sure if anyone else could have done what he did out there. Most of the attacks had been the regular Kresh, the attack dogs. Maybe a few soldiers. They sent one of their Mages, with Wraiths in tow. I don't even know how many of 'em. Then the rest had been Soldiers. They wrecked LA pretty bad."

"Very true," Polo said, "at least, until your boy got there. From all reports, he read 'em from the book."

"That he did," I said. "Not without some scratches, though. We lost more men, and he was beat up pretty bad too."

"He recovered quite well," Marco said. "I saw him a few days ago with the Archmage. He seemed to be holding up alright."

"He is," I said, "Losing men is always hard, and this was his first time in charge of something like that. He took the losses hard, but he's doin' better now."

"Taking losses is always hard, and should never become easy," Polomo said. "And how are you holding up after this last one? It was pretty rough on you, both in losses and other issues."

I knew he was talking about my Kresh heritage when he said other issues. The DNA inside my body was changing me. After touching their Source the changes had been faster. I thought I had known the depths of my rage until I had grabbed that Farrara'Ti by its Soul. My connection to their Source had begun there.

I am ashamed of what I did to that Soul before I let it go and it slid back through the Gateway. But it is a lesson learned. I can't use their Source, or I will become more and more like them.

"The losses aren't much easier to handle now than then," I said. "Not the least of which was the loss of Ric. The 'other' issues are there all the time, too, just beneath the surface. I have a huge weapon I could use against them, but to do so would destroy my humanity. I may become worse than those we face."

Marco and Polo had been two of the few people I had confided in after Second Kansas. They knew more about me than I ever wanted anyone to see. Unfortunately the cameras had been right on me when I'd ripped that Soul out of the Farrara'Ti, and the whole world saw what I did to it.

"That's why I pushed to get these weapons. I need something to face them with that can save me from having to do that."

"I don't know where the DNA is going to take you, Colin," Marco said, "but I seriously doubt it can completely change you from the man we see in front of us. Too much difference in your past, and the typical past of one of them to compare. Now I'm not sayin' to go out and use that particular skill, I'm just sayin' I can't see it turning you into worse than them."

"Thanks for the vote of confidence, but I don't think I want to put that to the test, if you don't mind," I said. "Much better to meet 'em with several hundred thousand Source weapons."

"So true," Polo agreed.

"Not to mention, Lyrica said she was gonna kick my ass if I even thought of touching their Source again."

"I have no doubt," Marcus said with a grin. "If there is one person who could, it would be that young lady."

Chapter 3

"You're extremely lucky things worked out as they did, Colin," Warren Grimes said.

Warren had been a Mage back when I was in the Academy. He'd gotten himself tied from the Source for abusing his power. As it turned out, he wasn't a bad guy. He couldn't do the things a Mage was supposed to do, so he'd chosen to arrange it where he didn't have to. It seemed to me like an extreme way to not do the fighting required of a Mage. But he still served the Soulguard in another capacity.

He'd been doing the financial wizardry that was putting Knoxville into a position of respect, instead of the place where the misfits were dropped.

When I got there I'd put my finances in his hands, and never regretted it for a moment.

"That's true," I said. "If it had failed, I would have had to move back in with Dad and Mom, and had to eat her cooking again."

"It wouldn't have been that drastic," He said with a chuckle, "but you would have been strapped for cash for a while as I built it back. Even with this war looming, I could have made money."

"I'm not sure I deserve you, man," I said, "but I sure am glad you're here."

"How did it go with the Archmage?"

"She was pissed," I answered.

"I thought she might be," he said. "The Guard has always wanted to be in charge of things, and they tend to get upset when someone else is setting the terms."

"Funny thing is," I said, "she wasn't mad about that. She was pissed because I didn't trust her enough to tell her about it til after the fact."

"That's a little surprising. I guess I'm still getting used to the new way things are being done since the change of the Council."

"Everything is different now," I said. "The war with Demons is completely different than it was for all those years. I'd say there have been more casualties on both sides in the last few years than the last five hundred totaled."

"I would agree," he said.

"And it's just a drop in the bucket of what's to come," I said. "My guys say there are hundreds of millions of Kresh on the home world. Just a small percentage are even aware that we exist. If we can't do somethin' pretty drastic, they'll roll over us with sheer numbers."

"Way to cheer a fellow up, boss," a voice came from behind us.

"What's up, Buddy?" I asked one of my oldest friends, Trent Deacons.

"Your better half sent me to ask if you still plan on dinner tomorrow with the usual suspects."

I looked at Warren, "I don't know. Am I broke?"

He chuckled, "No, you're not far from it, but with the success we've had with the project, you're ok. I'm sure you can afford one of those trips to Hooters."

"Looks like we're still on, then," I said as I turned back to Trent. "The good thing is I think it's all you can eat wings night tomorrow."

"Yeah," he said. "I can see that bein' pretty high on your list of important things to know. Right below the numbers of how many Kresh there are, is the schedule for all you can eat wings at Hooters."

"Not *right* below it."

He just looked at me with one eyebrow raised.

"Ok, maybe it is."

He laughed, "I thought so. I'll see ya later today then, Boss."

Warren was smiling as Trent walked away.

"It's good to see the sense of humor coming back, Sir," he said.

"Can't help it," I said. "If you can't laugh, what's it all worth?"

"True," he said. "When do we do our demonstration for the Archmage?"

"Friday," I answered, "along with Marco and Polo."

"You've been busy, then."

"Spent the whole day in meetings, so far," I said.

"Go on and do what you need to then," he said. "There's nothing new in your finances yet. After the demonstrations begin, on the other hand, that will change drastically."

"You know I don't want to profit from this..."

"We have a three percent mark-up, Sir," he said. "You'll make very little per gun, but we're looking at millions of sales if we are successful. That alone assures your financial future."

"Kinda hard to wrap my mind around that," I said.

"It may be, but you risked everything on this and it's about to pay off. Don't be ashamed of having a return. It could have very well failed, and you would have had to eat Kyra's cooking."

"Well, since you put it that way," I said with a laugh.

"I'll talk to you again before the demo, Sir"

"Seeya later, Warren."

***

"What the Hell are ya thinkin'?!" I heard Jacobs' voice all the way across the hangar. "You hit the powder, and the whole thing is gonna blow up in your face!"

He was yelling at a Mage fresh from the Academy. I could see the man had a Soulstream of about six inches in diameter. It was just as well, I'd seen this guy before, and he had the worst focus I've ever seen in a Mage. He was a support Mage and would never be more. Unlike Soulguards, Mages are born with their larger Soulstreams. There's not a whole lot you can do with a Mage who can't focus. They thought he might have enough focus to imbue the guns in a plane with the Source, but apparently not.

"I guess you're headin back to the Academy," he said at a slightly lower decibel. "Get your stuff, maybe you can go work with Lyrica. You don't need precision to help move patients around."

I walked over to the pair, and the young Mage made a quick exit.

Ivan Jacobs turned toward me and extended his hand. Or glove, you might say. During first Kansas, he'd lost his arm from the elbow down and his left leg from the knee down. I had helped him build a shield prosthesis for both. I had lit up his aura and Soulstream while he designed a very intricate shield to replace both lost appendages.

His invisible hand he kept inside a glove, so as not to freak out everyone around him. His hand gripped mine to my astonishment. It felt as normal as anyone's hand inside a glove. Maybe a little more solid, since the shield was harder than flesh would have been. What astonished me was the movement as he gripped my hand.

"That's impressive," I said. "You've got almost flawless mobility in the hand."

"It's like I was a child and learnin' to use the hand again. This time with mental nerves instead of physical," he said with a grin. "I still lose the mobility if there's too much goin on around me, but I'm getting better at it every day."

"I'm glad to hear that, Ivan," I said. "How are things goin on your front?"

"Looks like the AC-130 is comin' back, Boss," he said, "It was on a decline for years because there wasn't many places it could be used to its potential. Then you come along and give it a purpose again. You just gotta love these beasts."

"I liked the looks of 'em from the moment I first saw one," I said. "Speakin of which, have the new ones shown up yet? I need to do shields on em as soon as they get here."

"Saturday, they should be here."

"Good, I want as many of these things ready to go as we can get. I may not have the time to put shields on every one of 'em that the country has, but I want to shield as many as we can. I wish we could have come up with something a little simpler so that me and Lyr wouldn't have to do each one."

The air strip we had been using had grown quite a bit. At Second Kansas, there had been three AC-130s with Mages inside to imbue the weapons. We now had thirty five of them. Five were always kept crewed and ready at a moment's notice. There were also a bunch of assault helicopters, I couldn't remember what they were called but they had, what looked like a huge multi-barrel gun on the nose. I hadn't found a way to shield helos yet. They have too many parts that need to be free to move.

There were jets as well but, I was afraid to mess with the aerodynamics of something that fast. The jets bloould be used to drop all sorts of goodies into the middle of the next Demon horde that poked its nose out of the Kansas gate.

"It would be nice," he said, "but we play the cards we're dealt, Boss."

"So, I have a little good news for ya, buddy," I said. "She probably doesn't even know it yet, but

Gina is about to get transferred back here. She's done great at her first post in LA."

I saw the joy roll through his aura. I also saw a memory of Ivan buying a ring, and I smiled. That's one of the things that we have in common, amongst a few other things. We had both found the woman that completes us. He and Gina had been together from the moment she had gone home with him from the Hooters in Wichita. She had spent the last six months stationed in LA, though.

Due to the amount of new Soulguards, they would circulate through the posts much faster than we did when I was given my first post. I spent eight years in Knoxville as my first post. Now they do their first posting for six months, before being transferred to a more permanent station.

"That's the best news I've heard all week," he said. "I have a little surprise for her when she gets back."

"I bet you do," I said with a grin.

He looked at me with one eyebrow raised, "You been peekin'?"

He tapped the side of his head.

"Couldn't help it," I said. "You thought about it as soon as I said her name."

"Thank God she can't do that, I wouldn't ever get to surprise her with anything," He said, "How do you ever surprise Lyrica?"

"I never plan in advance," I said. "Surprises her all the time."

He laughed aloud.

"I've noticed that about ya, Boss. The good side is that the enemy won't figure out what ya got planned if ya just make shit up as ya go along."

"That's what I figured, and it's worked so far."

"True enough," he said with a smile.

Chapter 4

"What we got next, Boss?" Prada asked.

"Time to check out the new Mage cannons," I said. "You two should enjoy that."

My two escorts today were Galen Stone and Andrea Prada. Prada spent almost every day with me, just like before, but the others had begun cycling through soon after Second Kansas. I don't think I need a bodyguard, but they insist.

"I haven't had the pleasure of trying one of those yet," Stone said.

"There are ten new ones, and we'll be testin all of em'," I said.

"Nice," Prada said. "Those are fun."

"You just like shootin' stuff, Andrea," I said.

"Maybe," she returned, "but who's idea was it to make laser cannons that look like they come from a Star Wars movie?"

"I have no idea what you're talkin' about."

"Sure, go on and tell yourself that," she said. "At least you haven't made your swords glow like light sabers yet."

"Lyrica did that a long time ago, and Rictor never forgave her," I said.

The mention of my friend always brought with it a sadness, but it wasn't as bad as it had been several months back. For a time, I couldn't even think of Ric without going into a rage. I still feel that rage down inside, and there will come a time to release it. They'll come back again, and I'll let that beast from its cage. They call me Rash'Tor'Ri, the life ender. I intend to show them they chose the name well.

"True," she said. "He told all of us that if he saw one light saber, he was goin' to have the culprit on cleaning duty for a month."

"I remember that," I said with a chuckle. "Jacobs spent over three months cleanin' toilets. He said it was worth it though."

"It might have been worth it. I saw Ric's face when Jacobs did it the first time. It was just... utter despair. It was priceless. He grumbled for hours. You would hear a word or two every so often. 'Jaegher' was one of the most frequent. 'Friggin Rourkes' was another."

"I don't see why I got blamed."

She snorted, "You gave orders in 'Yoda' speak for a month after she did that."

"Incorrect in your recollections, certain I am."

Stone laughed aloud.

We had been walking out toward the Gate, and it had changed a great deal since Second Kansas. There were so many guns surrounding the gateway, it would be hard to count. There were shields around raised platforms with what looked like laser cannons mounted on top all over the place. The ten new weapons were on the East side so we headed that direction.

"All right," I said as we reached the platform of the first new gun, "go ahead Stone. You're familiar with the process?"

"I've watched others fire them," he said with a nod, "but I just haven't done it myself."

He jumped up on the platform.

The difference between these and a regular gun, would be the ammo. These had no magazine, or power source. They are fueled by a Mage's Soullance. There are shield lenses inside to focus and concentrate the fire into, basically, a laser. It makes a support Mage able to fire a shot that can take out a Wraith. A powerful Mage can do some serious damage with one of these.

This is the same concept I used with the Source weapons. We tried to make lenses out of glass, but the Source doesn't work like light, exactly. I had to design shield lenses for the barrels. This is going to be the production chokepoint when we start truly producing the guns. This is why I need Mages. They don't need to be strong, just focused.

This is actually not hard to find. Most support Mages weren't powerful, and had made up for it in precision. Some, like the fellow Jacobs had been yelling at, were almost useless. The only thing they are good for is support in making shields. No precision needed to do that except for the lead Mage.

The hair stood up on the back of my neck, and my teeth seemed to vibrate as Galen Pulled from the Source. I watched as he channeled it into his lance, and fired it into the cannon where a ten inch gout of Soulfire was focused into a two inch beam of concentrated Hell. It ripped the ground out by the Gate, and left a trail of melted rock.

Stone had a huge grin on his face, as he passed the weapon back and forth across the area in front of it.

I couldn't even imagine what it would look like if Paige fired one of these. There's no guarantee the gun could even handle that much power it might just melt. She's afraid to use it much. One slip with that sort of power, and the explosion that Nora Kestril had created at First Kansas would look like child's play.

Paige or I could go through one of these gates and Mage bomb. We could end this war in one fell swoop. We've both talked about doing just that. But if we do, it means we give up on fourteen other worlds of human life out there in the same position as we are, or worse.

Now, with what had happened in Romania, it was even worse for me. I have marked others with the telepathic Mark that I gained from my Kresh DNA. They are my "subjects" you might say. The closest thing I can figure, they are sworn to my service, and I am responsible for them. And I am responsible for thousands of humans on Kresh and other worlds, along with several million actual Kresh.

I can't just turn my back on them, so we prepare for a long, bloody war.

As Stone finished playing and jumped down, Prada who had been watching started toward the next one.

"My turn," she said with a disturbing smile.

It's probably a good thing I wasn't watching her Soul. I think I may have rubbed off on some of my friends. I get a disturbing amount of joy from sheer destruction. As a matter of fact, I planned to use a couple of the guns as well.

***

We had spent several hours firing the guns, and I had sent my escort on back to the base. I liked to spend a little time out at the Gateway by myself every day.

I took my mp3 player from my pocket, and affixed it to my shoulder with a small shield. The earbuds were held in place by a small set of shields as well. I had gone through several players, by moving so fast that they were slung from pockets to shatter, before I had started working out this way.

I pushed play, and the grinding guitar and growling voice of Metallica's lead singer pounded in my ears.

My music makes most folks just shake their heads. I love the rage music, and it helps me bleed off the huge well of rage inside me. I genuinely feel better after listening to a song filled with rage.

I drew my twin swords from the sheaths on my back and began the Dance of Blades, the fluid like changing from stance to stance. Kyra had trained me from the time I could carry a toy sword in this dance. I'm actually one of the few who are considered Master level in the art. Kyra makes the dance look beautiful, Lyrica does the same. Most folks say my dance is scary, probably due to the rage I can bleed off with it. It looks like concentrated fury. I tend to lose myself in the rage as I practice. I usually do my daily session out by the gate.

A few hours later, with Maria Brink, from In This Moment screaming in my ears, I came to rest with a final stance. I was covered in sweat, and the great reservoir of rage inside me was noticeably less. If I didn't do this daily, I'm afraid I would blow up.

I sheathed my swords and started back toward the base. Lyrica and I shared a place in the residences at the far side of the base. She'd been working in Wichita all day at the hospital. That's where she spent most days.

If I needed her here for special projects, she would come. But her passion was for healing. She is so much better than me. I think, all the time, of ways I can destroy. She thinks of new ways she can heal others. I don't really understand how she can love me as she does when we are so different.

As I passed the Guards on station I got a few waves, which I returned. I always hear comments that they are unaware I can hear.

"Out at the Gate again..."

"Whatcha think he does out there?"

"Probably hoping they'll show up while he's out there."

Its scary how close to the truth that one was. Sometimes I wish the gate would open while I'm at ground zero.

"Were you here at Second Kansas?"

"No, they say he ripped the Soul right out of one of 'em."

"He did. I was there. He..."

I frowned to myself as I walked out of range. I could have boosted my hearing, but I didn't really want to hear more of that conversation. It always seemed to come down to that. The one thing I am most ashamed of is the thing that sticks with everyone's memories.

It doesn't help that the television played that footage for months as its top story. The great invasion is at hand, and then that scene and "we have the Soulguard to protect us" stories.

There had been a lot of "Rourke not available for comment" in the reports. I tend to avoid the press. Even Jennifer Alstead had stopped asking for my story as a piece to build up the Soulguard. She had kept asking for some time but my steadfast refusal had finally sunk in to her brain. She was still the one who covered most stories about us, and I had done several interviews with her. But she stayed away from some of the things she knew bothered me the most.

Unfortunately, this was just the beginning of what I believed would be the bloodiest war our planet had ever seen. If the Kresh ever get their shit settled we are done for. I hoped they'd never get it together. Our only chance was if they kept coming at us piecemeal as they'd done so far. If they ever got truly unified, they'd run over us with numbers alone.

Chapter 5

"More wings, please," I answered the waitress that had just returned to our table for the fifth time.

She craned her neck to see over Kharl. She looked at me with one eyebrow raised.

"Where are you putting all of those?" she asked. "You got a hollow leg or something?"

"I'm pretty sure he does," Lyrica answered her.

"He must have," she said with a shake of her head. "That's four plates of wings.

"I could see one of these two," she motioned toward Kharl and Dietrich who almost took up the whole side of the tables that were pulled together. Kyra was almost invisible sitting between the two giants. "But then they're both big as a house."

"But I work harder, so I have to eat more," I said. "Those two always just stand around orderin' people to do the work."

Dietrich's sneeze sounded disturbingly like 'bullshit', but I knew that couldn't be the case.

"Now that ya mention it," Kharl rumbled, "I could use another plate of wings too."

Dietrich smiled and nodded to the waitress as well, "Definitely need more."

She left as several eyes followed her. There were two grunts as a couple of blows landed and I laughed. I had been smart enough not to look at her, so Lyrica hadn't been one of those who had kidney punched two men. Kharl and Trent were both favoring their left sides.

Mattie and Trent had become an item over the last few months and Lyrica had been as happy as she could be. She'd been saying they should just get a room for years.

"So has anyone heard about the attempted bank robbery they had in town last month?"

I groaned as Jacobs asked that question. Lyrica giggled. I couldn't hide that from her anyway. I hadn't told anyone else about it.

It just so happened that Jacobs had witnessed the whole thing. He'd been waiting for a month to tell this at one of the gatherings it seemed. It was a tradition of sorts to tell some story about the antics of a certain Soullord.

"Well," he said with a grin, "Let me tell ya all about it."

"The illustrious potentate and I were at the east branch of Capitol Federal, which happens to be the bank where most Soulguards do their business now.

"In walk these four guys. They looked suspicious to me, although our Boss doesn't even pay any attention. He's busy at the teller countin' out all that money he has."

Actually, I had been there seeing if I could afford to buy my lunch.

"Anyway, these guys draw guns and start screamin'. Now I don't wanna be insulting to 'em, but if you're gonna rob a bank, would ya choose the one that has Soulguards in it at almost any given time?

"I don't think I would. But that's exactly what these geniuses did. Finally the boss looks up from his bucket full of hundred dollar bills and sees what's goin on."

Fourteen dollars and thirty-two cents.

"We all turn around as their leader screams 'Nobody move and nobody gets hurt!'"

"As it turned out this guy was pointin' his gun at this lady and her kid. Our intrepid leader freaked out. I mean fiery eyes, death to all, and all that."

He had a point, cause I did lose it for a minute. I had seen this guy's Soul, and I could feel that he wanted to kill. He wanted to kill that little girl, and I couldn't abide that. Children are sacred, they are our future and should be protected at all costs.

"Next thing anyone knows, this guy is dangling off the floor by his neck, and you can feel all this 'I want to kill you' comin' from that side of the bank.

"He says, 'Where's the fun in that?' so the guy wets his pants, and the boss regains a little composure and stuffs the guy in a trash can. All you can see stickin' out of the trash can is a head and two feet.

"With all this goin' on, I just figured 'What the hell?' and grabbed the nearest one to me and stuffed him in another trash can.

"Then we moved on over and grabbed the other two. There was only one more trash can, and I got to it first, so I stuffed mine inside the can and laughed at him."

"I'm almost afraid to ask what he did with the other one," Kharl said.

"Well, you'd think scotch tape wouldn't really hold a guy."

"Good lord," Kyra said. "How much tape would that even take?"

"Seventy-four rolls," I answered.

***

The C-130 was loud and Prada looked pissed. She always looked pissed when we were in an airplane for some reason.

We all had our coms attached so we could speak even with the noise.

"So what we're lookin' for is a unified jump," I said. "There are seven colored targets on the ground in a circular formation. Then there is a center target where I will try to land with two squads. You each have a color on the wristband. After we are airborne, you start getting your bearings and go for your color. I want as tight a formation as you can get."

"Combat drop or just a drop?" Cristof Damaris asked.

"The first will be a basic drop," with a grin.

"First?" Prada asked.

"Oh yeah," I said with a grin. "We got the plane all day, and we're gonna take advantage of it."

I could see her muttering something about "Friggin' Soullords" at the other end of the craft with her Mageguards.

Mageguard is the term we use for one of the Guards who have gone through the Ascension process with either Lyrica or myself. Their Soulstreams are Mage strength, but they haven't been through the courses at the Academy to begin instruction on how to properly Pull the Source. They have the strength and speed of a Mage with the skills of a Guard.

Kharl had shown the power of the Mageguard in the demonstration we had done for the American Government that seemed like a long time ago.

We had ascended every Guard that had come in with my merry band of misfits. Each Mage had ten Mageguards now. We had been working together for the last six months every chance we got. This just happened to be a day when we could use the planes to practice drops.

As we neared our target, each Mage looked at their wristband and where their target had been placed. I saw Prada muttering again.

The door opened and the light flashed red. Green would mean to jump. The nearest squad approached the door, Reyna Sereno and her ten. Directly behind her squad was Galen Stone and his. Len Yueh was next, then Prada, Alexei Rostov, Cristof Damaris, Adaya Tovah, Alec Brighton, Asante Xhosa, and Lennox Flynn bringing up the rear.

The light turned green and Rheyna dived out the back with her guys. As Stone jumped with his I could hear Prada muttering again.

As she got closer I could hear her.

"Where's that son of a bitch when you need him?"

"Who?" Rostov asked from behind her.

"Rictor Freakin Hughes!" she yelled back just as she got to me.

I threw her out of the plane.

As Rostov got close to me he was still laughing.

I shrugged and, since I needed to gather both of my squads who would hit center with me, I jumped on out of the plane too.

I dived toward the two squads who would land with me in the center. Both Prada and Rostov were already arranging their groups where they needed to be. I ended my dive by flattening my body out to catch more wind and placed myself in the center.

Rostov was on my left and Prada to the right. When I looked at her she was looking the other way, but she was telling me what she thought of my actions with a rude hand gesture.

I laughed.

This one was infinitely easier than the combat drop. Combat drop didn't use shield chutes. The combat drop involves the two squads who jump with me. They are linked to me, so I can draw power, and I have a shield platform that we are all on top of. It took me a while to perfect the platform without it flipping and dumping us, but I finally got it right.

We go down as fast as possible and then at my signal, the two Mages Pull and I snatch the power. Add that to my own and channel it through the shield, and we have power to brake the shield platform. Once it slows enough, I just turn it off and we drop the rest of the way. Naturally, Prada hates that one even worse than the chute drop. Alec on the other hand loves it.

That's why I let her squad and Alec's squad do it a second time at the end of the day when I found out we had time for an extra flight.

Chapter 6

Lyrica was working late at the hospital in Wichita, so I was pretty much left to my own devices on Thursday night. We'd spent all day jumping out of the plane, and I was a little antsy.

The proto-type was ready for the demonstration on Friday, so I didn't really have much to do. And I didn't have a bunch of money, so there wasn't going to be a restaurant visit.

Finally I decided to go for a run. I put the earbuds in for my mp3 player and cranked it up. Godsmack pounded in my ears as I took off at a moderate fifty miles per hour or so.

I headed back out toward the Gate. I spend a lot of time out there, I guess. As I began circling the area, I took notice of all the guns we had in place. There were various types of cannons set up in a ring around the field. They were built on platforms so that the fire could be kept angled down into the horde. These would have grape shot and support Mages to light up the barrels.

There were Mage cannons all over the place for use as the opportunity arose. Back at the base was an artillery station for bombardment.

Then there was the airstrip with the AC-130s and the assault helos. I don't think we could get much more prepared for the bastards.

There were thirteen thousand Soulguards stationed at the base, which had grown to take in the majority of Hillsboro, along with close to twenty five thousand National Guardsmen. Our ranks were growing all over the world as people saw what had happened here in Kansas and the attacks on major cities in the US.

I felt it doubtful that they would come back to Kansas with their next wave, and so did most of the people I knew. But we would be prepared if it did happen.

I had been lost in thought and almost ran over my Mom, as I turned around a corner.

"For someone who can see as much as you do," she said as we both stopped, "that was awful close."

"I wasn't payin attention, Mom," I answered with a grin. "Lost in thought, I guess."

"I can see that," she said. "There's a lot to think about, nowadays."

"How's Lyr?" she asked.

"Happy as could be," I answered. "She amazes me on an hourly basis. She's at the hospital at the moment. She said she had a few patients that needed a little more than the rest, and she wanted to stay late to take care of 'em."

"Doesn't surprise me," Kyra said. "She was always a sweet kid, and she's turned into a wonderful woman."

"I honestly don't know what I'd do without her."

Kyra smiled, "She set her sights on you as soon as you saved her in Knoxville."

"She was six," I said.

"She knew, even back then."

"I guess so."

"Did you know," Kyra asked, "she refused to take the official Oath?"

"No I didn't," I answered. "Why'd she refuse?"

"She said there wouldn't be any damn oath to keep her from doing whatever she had to do to keep you safe."

That sent a chill down my spine. Lyrica Jayne is a wonderful person. A person who shows a kindness to others that I couldn't even hope to match. But when the Council had gone off the deep end and tried to kill me, and later try to kill Gregor, she had destroyed them all.

I can't fault her for not taking the Oath. It is a great inconvenience at times. There are monsters both Human and Kresh. I had skirted the edge of my Oath several times in the past.

"That sounds like Lyrica," I said.

"Yes it does," she agreed.

"I do have a question for you," I said, "on a totally different subject."

"What's that?"

"Guards were able to craft shields for themselves," I said. "What are the chances those same guards can create shields on a smaller scale for a project I am working on?"

"What do you mean?"

"Can a Guard connect a small shield to the Source like a Mage does?"

"I'm not certain how a Mage does that," she said, "but who knew we could craft shields at all? I'd certainly be willing to try something new if it would prove useful."

"Very useful, indeed," I said.

"Then I'll try it, if you want me to."

"Tomorrow," I said, "we have a demonstration for the Archmage and our two Generals. If you don't mind, come out to the meeting as well. We'll give it a try after I show you what they'd be for. If Guards can do that part, then it will free up a lot of Mages for the main tie-in of the gun."

"Gun?"

"We've devised a Source Weapon, and I need to put some serious time into production if this demo is successful."

"You never cease to amaze me, Son," she said. "All those years of everyone trying to hide their skills from everyone else, and no new innovations. Then we throw a seventeen year old into the room, and everything blows up. I am very proud of you."

She hugged me and said, "I'll definitely be there tomorrow, and I'll bring some others I think may help. Focus is the main thing we need, is it not?"

"Yeah, the better they are at focusing the better the job will go. Thanks, Mom."

"You're welcome," she said. "Now get back to running or you'll get flabby."

She jogged off the way she had been running, and began to pick up speed. I returned to my run as well.

If I could use Guards to make the lenses in the barrels of the weapons, it would take less Mages for the whole process. Guards were much more plentiful in numbers than Mages.

Not for lack of trying, though. Lyrica and I average fifty new Mageguards a week. They are going through the Academies as fast as we can run them through. When I joined the Academy, there had been about nine hundred Mages. Now there was close to four hundred new Mages, and another eight hundred Mageguards.

Sunday we were lined up to add another fifty Mageguards to the ranks. We take volunteers only, and they must have enough skill at focusing to survive the process. Among the fifty new volunteers were Trent Deacons and Mattie Riordan.

I had no doubt in either of my friends, as both could handle what focus was necessary to ascend.

I continued running around the battlefield, and my thoughts inevitably turned to my friend. He'd been one of the few people who knew me from before things went crazy. It seemed there were fewer and fewer of those people.

I turned another bend in my route, and saw someone waiting down the path. It was one of the Shak'Tar. Not one of the several who had stayed with me when the others went back with Gorvelis. It took me a moment to remember his name.

"Fero Jintera," I said as I approached, "if I remember correctly."

I saw his smile and felt the rush of happiness that I had remembered his name. I had met him once for about ten minutes. It was soon after Second Kansas. He had brought me a report of the success that Touran Gorvelis had accomplished on Cerres, one of the colonies that were held by the Kresh.

I also saw Pelin approaching. She had sensed the new presence faster than I had.

"Master," he said with a nod, "I have come with messages."

"It's good to see you still kickin' Fero," I said. "How goes the war on Cerres?"

"Very good, Master," he said.

"You don't have to call me Master, Fero."

"He tries to get us not to call him that too, Fero," Pelin said as she walked over, "but pay it no mind. One day, he'll just accept it."

Fero chuckled. He didn't seem as awestruck as last time and I, for one, am glad of it. It gets old having people look at you that way.

"What messages do you have for me, Fero?" I asked with a grin.

"The first is from Gorvelis, Master," he said. "Cerres is ours. We have taken the last village, and all on the planet are Marked."

"What?" I asked with a chill sliding up my spine. "Everyone is Marked?"

"Yes, Master. Both Human and Kresh are of the clan of Rash'Tor'Ri," he said, proudly.

I was stunned, and horrified.

"What is it, Master?" Fero asked. "Why are you displeased?"

"I don't want to Mark anyone, Fero," I said. "I want them to be free."

He looked at me in confusion. Pelin placed her hand on his shoulder.

"Our Master is not displeased with you, Fero," she said. "He is of a world that does not know the Mark."

She passed him a huge amount of knowledge in a sudden burst of her telepathy. His eyes widened in total surprise.

After she was done he turned to me again, "I must go back immediately, and show Touran what it is you are asking of us. It is too late to stop the Mark in Cerres. But He will know what to do."

I was still stunned.

"You have a second message for the Master?" Pelin asked.

"Yes," he said, still flustered by the concept of freedom. "A Farrara'Ti intercepted me before I could get through the Gate to Doran, your Earth. He wishes to speak with Rash'Tor'Ri. He will come here on a date and time set by you. He will come alone. His name is Kil'Sin'Deres."

I was speechless for a moment, as I ran that through my head a few times. Why would Kil'Sin'Deres want to speak to me? Why would he trust me enough to put himself that far in my power? What could he want?

"Master" Pelin interrupted my thoughts, "all of those questions can be asked of Kil'Sin'Deres when he comes. You must give him a date and time."

My thoughts may just have well been words with two telepaths standing in front of me.

"Five days from now, I'll meet him at the spot we first met, at dusk," I said. "Tell Gorvelis that we don't Mark any other Humans. If you don't tell him anything else, you remember that, Fero."

"Yes, Master," he said.

I even forgot to tell him not to call me Master. There was so much in what he'd just told me that I didn't know what to do.

"Get him fed before he heads back, Pelin," I said, still in a daze.

What the Hell do I do now? There were thirty million people on Cerres, if my reports had been accurate from the Shak'Tar. I knew he had Marked the Kresh. I had no idea he had Marked the whole damn planet.

And what the Hell did Kil'Sin'Deres want? Like things weren't complicated enough on Earth.

Chapter 7

Paige answered the door to her residence on base to see me standing there with a dazed expression on my face.

"Oh, my god," she said immediately, "what's happened?"

"I have a serious problem," I said, "and no idea what I can do about it."

After I told her the night's events, she just sat there for what seemed like an eternity as she thought.

"I knew this Mark business was going to come back and bite you, but this is enormous," she said. "The first thing we do is get Lyrica here. She needs to know, immediately. You should have gone to her before coming here, anyway."

"She is still at the hospital," I said, "or that would have been the first place I would have gone."

"Ok," she said. "Next, how can you possibly protect this other world while you are on this one?"

"Perhaps my meeting with Kil'Sin'Deres will help on that score," I said, "I really have no idea what he wants. Maybe I could convince him to move into the facility for that world."

"That's if he's still an ally, or if he ever was an ally."

"True," I said, "because he's never really declared where he was standing. He did take in my clans when they were Marked in Romania, so I'm hoping he is an ally."

"The fact that he is coming here alone to meet you looks good for that theory," she said, "but we won't know for sure until then."

"This is true," I said, "but I need some sort of plan, and I think I'm still in shock."

"My first suggestion would be this," she said. "You are now the sole ruler of a world. It's crazy but it seems to be the fact of the matter. What I will do is ask this ruler to allow the Soulguard to set up an Academy on this world. We can bring them a defense they would get nowhere else."

I felt a huge swell of relief as I thought of it. There is no one in this world or another who could learn to become a Soulguard faster than a telepath. They are already sworn to me, and I am under Oath to the Soulguard. Perhaps we could, together, do something positive for those people.

"We would need someone who we trust implicitly," I said. "They would have to be pretty strong as well, and well-liked by the men and women who would be goin' with them."

"Someone who could not be corrupted by the power we would be placing in his or her hands. Someone who has been allied with you from almost the beginning."

"You've got someone in mind, don't you?" I asked.

Immediately I saw two different faces flash through her memories.

"I think they would be great choices," I said, "But I'm worried about Darrel."

Darrel Barnes had been out there at First Kansas with us. He'd been a support for me as I used the power of over two hundred Soulguards to shut down a Gate. He had been given a seat on the Council but, what had happened out there had traumatized him, I think. He avoided me like the plague. He could barely even look at me without his aura flooding with the fear he had felt out there.

"He's a good man, Colin," she said. "He just has a relentless fear of you."

"I know," I said. "That's what I'm afraid of. We're sending him out into the middle of thousands of telepaths that are Marked to try to be like me."

"I still think he could handle that," she said.

"Ok," I said. "You'd know better than I would. He hasn't spoken to me since First Kansas. The first choice is dead on. Sam would be ideal for something like this. If he's willing, I think he'd do great."

Sam Keller had been the first Mage Captain I had met in Knoxville, and he'd taught me a lot before he was moved out. After he'd gotten New York as his next post, we'd kept in touch. He also followed me to First Kansas in defiance of direct orders not to. When things settled, he, also, was given a seat on Paige's new Council.

"I might need to do something to make him powerful enough so as not to raise a stink with the other Mages he might be bypassing."

"I doubt that," she said. "They won't want a posting like this. To them it would be a sentence to

Hell. Start an Academy amidst thirty million people who want to be just like you."

I snorted, "I guess you got a point there."

"Now," she said, "You should go home and let Gregor and I hash this out. Make sure your gun works, and let's get this thing started so we can hurt them when they come back."

"That I can do," I said, "and I still have to tell Lyr about this. Last time she said I had given her a hard time because she brought home a dog. Lord knows what she'll want to bring home now. How could I even say no?"

***

"I think I better not ever hear another bad comment about my dog," Lyrica said after sitting quietly through my summary of the day.

She had watched it in my memories as I told her the events.

"That's all you got to say about it?"

"It sounds like Paige said most of the important stuff," she said, "so, yeah, that's about it."

"I love you," I said, "and I won't give ya any more grief about your ugly, smelly dog."

"What did I just say?"

"Truth is truth baby. He's definitely ugly, and he smells like he ate the south end of a northbound skunk."

"One more word," she said, "just one more, and I'm opening the door so he can come climb on the bed with us."

I cringed.

"That beautiful, sweet animal."

She laughed her melodic laughter that I loved more than anything.

Chapter 8

"The weapon, itself is a pretty simple design," I said. "The stock is a simple, shaped composite. The Source doesn't actually connect to that part, so the electronics inside are relatively safe from damage on that front."

Each of them held a black piece of composite, roughly shaped like the stock of a rifle with grips for hand holds. There was a slot on the bottom about three inches in diameter.

"Inside this piece is the circuitry that makes the whole thing work. There is no access to this part. It's a solid mold around the parts so it's water-proof, shock proof, and all that. You can throw it on the ground and not hurt it. Very durable."

I picked up the next section of the four parts to the weapon system.

"This is the barrel," I said. "It's roughly the size of a large shotgun barrel. Maybe a little bigger. It's made of hardened steel. Inside the barrel is a focusing lens. It focuses the three inch stream that is released into the barrel to a one and a half inch stream. This makes the barrels last quite a bit longer, since they don't have to squeeze it down with channeling through the metal tubes."

"The third piece is the part that is connected to the Source by a shield that is shaped like a six inch soul stream."

I lit up the shield that had been made by Jacobs. I wanted a Mage to do it and Jacobs was more than happy to do it. It was just a shield tube that fed itself with two small tendrils down into the ground.

"It wasn't too complicated for our test Mage to build and it serves as a channel for the Source to follow as the weapon is activated. The Source will follow the easiest path when that happens and we just gave it a shortcut."

The piece looked like a plumbing reducer, to be honest.

"It's also made of hardened steel," I said, "and inside is another shield lens. This focuses the six inch down to a three inch as it enters the clip or magazine."

"Now the most important part." I picked up a combat helmet.

"Inside this helmet is the key to make the whole thing work. When someone puts on the helmet, the tech inside is scanning their brain, and sending an exact replica to the gun. In effect making the gun a living being."

The guy who had tested the gun for me stepped forward. John Hiner was an ex-Air Force mechanic I had run into some time back. He'd volunteered to test the gun from the beginning, and had shot it several times already.

As I handed the helmet to John, I lit up the shields so everyone could see them. John placed the helmet on his head, and held the gun stock. The shield to the clip was still a shield. He then snapped the barrel in place.

He lifted the clip and slid it into the bottom of the gun with a click. As soon as it clicked, the connection from the helmet to gun reached the conduit to the Source.

"Holy shit!" Polo said, "look at that."

The Source had taken the easiest route to the gun which was the shielded tube already in place. For all intents and purposes the gun now had a six inch Soulstream.

"Now John tells me it's pretty easy to tell when that happens, and it's not too hard to learn to Pull the Source. Unlike a Mage, it's not going to get past the focus, and reach the body. Basically anyone can use it, focus or not."

"Where a Mage can use the Source for all sorts of things, this has just a single way to use it. But an effective way."

"Fire it up, John."

As John fired the weapon, he braced himself. An inch and a half of pure hell hit the target about a hundred yards out, and ripped it to shreds.

"It's got a kick to it," I said, "He wasn't braced for it the first time he shot it, and landed on his ass."

As he finished firing the gun, John stepped back to the table, and unclipped the magazine. As it slipped free the Soulstream was gone, leaving just the shield it had before.

"That," Marco said, "is impressive. Your first contract will be signed before the day is out."

"I'll have to put you with Warren Grimes on that part," I said. "After all, I just blow stuff up."

"I see a rude surprise for the Kresh if we can get these out there in time," Paige said.

"I certainly hope so," I said. "That's the idea."

Kyra and several Guards stood at the back of the group. Kyra had a huge grin on her face. We owe the Kresh so much for what they have done to all of us. It's so nice to be a part of the paying back of that debt. A debt of blood and death. This would just be a small part of the Hell I planned to bring to them.

"You'll have whatever you need," Paige said, "Mages, and Guards. Just let us know."

"They'll be paid for their efforts," I said. "Support Mages will be fine, and we're about to find out if Guards can make the small shields for the lenses. I'll get back to ya on that."

"For the actual work we have planned," I said as Kyra approached, "Warren has some guys settin up a holograph projector for the lenses we need."

"I don't see any reason we can't make these lenses," Kyra said. "The shield around the stream might be a possibility as well. You may be able to use Guards for all of it, with as small of feeders that we're dealing with."

"Now that would be great," I said. "Our Mages are stretched thin as it is. Speakin' of Mages, when are you planning to do the deed and join the Mageguards, Mom?"

"Hell, Son," she said with a shake of her head, "I'm just a teacher, now."

"You should come out Sunday, anyway," I said. "You can join the others we're goin to raise."

"I'll think about it," she said.

"You should," Paige said. "You are needed where you are, regardless of Guard or Mage strength. And when the ship hits the sand, you're more powerful than you were before. Every bit helps."

"Not to mention," I said, "if Dad gets mouthy, you can throw him through a wall."

"Now that is a valid argument," she said.

***

Sunday was a beautiful, sunny day. Perfect for burning the sky. It never seemed to fail, any time Lyrica or I did this particular act, there would be a lot of spectators. A couple of Senators had actually flown in to see this one.

"Senator Deacons," I said as Trent's father approached, "how are you today?"

"Doing well, Colin," he said. "I understand you are doing this ascension process on my boy today. I thought I should come and see it in action. I've heard about it numerous times."

"He's ready for it," I said, "I wouldn't do it, otherwise."

"I've trusted you for years, Colin," he said, "and I don't see a reason not to trust you now. He trusts you, and I will, too."

"We're careful, sir."

He nodded and headed toward his seat under a canopy that had been set up for VIPs.

Of course it's dangerous to do what we do, but we had a pretty good handle on it since we did this every week. It still looks damned impressive though when one of us Pulls that much power.

The first five of my group stepped forward and my support Mages opened their portals on the tether that we formed between us some time back.

Today there were five of my ten Mages from my own squad. Damaris, Tovah, Rostov, Xhosa, and of course Prada. I felt the Source start flowing into me as I lit the five Soulguards' Streams up, as well as mine.

"This is what I need you to form," I said as I showed them the shield tube that led out of my stream and pointed to the sky. "Don't let any into you, steer it out that tube."

I looked at each, received their nod, and watched all five form the tube I asked for.

"And don't touch it after the Pull until you get some classes in. With the backlog we have at the Academies, you'll just be using the strength and shield benefit for some time."

When they were ready, I Pulled gently through their streams, and I felt the Source being pulled into my body from the links to my Mages. I don't have a clue why it's like this, but it is.

Perhaps there is some sort of balance that has to be met. Who knows, it just is what it is.

After watching to be sure they were channeling the power away from themselves, I Pulled harder.

Soulfire Poured into the sky in five gouts. The harder I Pulled, the larger the gouts of fire became. This time I stopped before they reached the outer limits of their stream to hold the power.

We had learned that a Soulstream that is about fifteen inches in diameter was much easier to learn to use than some of the ones I had done earlier on. A Stream like Gregor's would be a beast to learn to use, if you had come straight from Soulguard to Mage.

So that's where we stopped our Pulls under most circumstances. There were a few that we would take further, such as Mom. Her Stream was huge for a guard because of her age. When we ascend an Elite, we tend to take them further.

"Don't play with it or you'll go blind," I said to the new Mageguards in front of me.

"They used to always tell me that," Alex Campbell, one of the new Mageguards said, "but it's all lies."

"I don't know," I said with a chuckle, "'cause I heard of this guy over in Scotland..."

Chapter 9

I was back on the dark plains where I had fought the hordes of darkness in my Source Coma.

This time I was not alone. All around me were my friends, my family. All of the people I cared for stood with me on the plains.

The darkness began to close in and I felt immobilized. I couldn't do anything as those on the outskirts of my dream fell away from us into that darkness.

My rage beat at my senses as the darkness grew ever closer. I saw my friends Trent and Mattie fall, and I screamed. I saw Rictor tumble into the darkness.

Closer and closer it came and more and more it consumed until it seemed within arms' reach. I still couldn't move, and my screams became inhuman roars.

Kharl and Kyra, Paige, Gregor, all fell from the tiny precipice where I was held.

Something cold and hate-filled came out of that dark spot in my soul.

I was staring into Lyrica's green eyes as she fell away from me into that darkness, and that Presence inside me came striding out of the dark spot. Every step shook the ground below me and when it stepped forth, Power came with it.

I came awake with power blasting upwards through the roof of the house Lyrica and I shared. My roar of fury didn't even sound human. It reverberated through the cluster of residences where we were housed on base.

It felt like a vice settled around me as Lyrica grabbed me. She grabbed the power I was Pulling and threw it skyward. I finally got control of myself as the dream receded, and so did the awful presence of that monster inside of me.

The dream had felt so real but now the cold hate was replaced with shame.

"It's ok, my heart," soft words in my ear.

Her hand stroked the side of my head as I fought with the rage inside me that sprang from the shame of not being able to control myself enough to even have a nightmare.

I didn't know what sparked that nightmare. Perhaps the eminent meeting with Kil'Sin'Deres had done it. But the roof of the house certainly paid a hefty price for it.

"Maybe we should just sleep outside," Lyrica said, "of course then they would get a show from bedtime explosions of one sort and morning explosions of another."

"Wouldn't that look good on a television report?" I said and looked up, "It seems we need a new roof."

"It would appear," she said as she lay back and looked up, "though I did always like skylights."

***

"Should I come with you?" Lyrica asked.

We were in Montana where there still was a Soulguard presence. The Academy had moved back there to train new Mages since there were so many new Mages to train.

Paige and Gregor were still in Kansas, but they had left a goodly part of the Council in Montana for any major decision making. Darrel Barnes was acting as, I guess it would be called Dean of the Academy.

He hadn't come to meet me, but Sam Keller had been waiting on the edge of the runway as we landed.

"I think I need to do this alone, Honey," I answered. "He is putting a lot of trust in us not to attack. I should give him the same respect, I suppose."

"Probably so," she said with a frown. "But I still think you get in too much trouble when you go off all alone."

"You do have a point there," a voice came from our right.

Sam Keller had walked over from the side of the runway.

"I'd say he shouldn't even be let out of the house without a chaperone," he said with a grin.

"That hurts my feeling, Sam," I said. "It cuts me deep."

"I'm sorry about your one feelin', but truth is truth."

"Amen!" Lyrica chimed in.

"Et tu Brute'," I said.

"Damn skippy, me too," she said, "but you call me *Brutus* one more time and it's on."

Sam laughed aloud, "I certainly miss you two around here. It's just not the same."

"Yeah right," I said, "but you just wait till you hear what's in store for you in the future."

"That sounds ominous," he said with a serious tone. "Is this something I'm gonna like?"

"Depends on you," I said. "If it was me, I'd be thrilled. But I'm a little nuts after all."

"Damn, quit holdin' me in suspense," he said, "and spit it out."

"There's about to be an opening for a very important job," I said. "Let's retire to the cafeteria and I'll tell you all about it."

Fifteen minutes later, as we waited for our food to get ready, I told him what had happened and the solution that Paige had suggested.

"Ain't that a Hell of a thing," he said. "You're serious about this?"

"Afraid so, Sam," I said. "I really wish they hadn't Marked those people, but it is what it is, and I have a responsibility to them. Paige thinks it is a good idea, and we get a whole new army of Soulguards ready to join the fight. Or to hold their ground till we finish here."

"That involves one great big assumption, Colin," Sam said.

"Yes it does," I said.

"Can we win here?"

"We have to," I said, "and I'll be going under that assumption until they read me my Last Rites and burn my bones."

"I see," he said. "I can understand where I would be a fair choice for this. I got no family left here, but the Guard is my family now. Barnes is in a different position though. He's got family and I don't know whether he would want to leave them behind."

"See, this is where Paige and Gregor are hashing out details. We're possibly talkin' about relocating whole families if it's what they want."

"Hmmm," he said, "well, I'm interested, but I have to have a lot more detail before I jump in the water."

"That's to be expected, and I'm workin on getting more details about Cerres before this begins. I told Paige I would sound you out on the subject while I'm here."

"And just why are you here?" he asked. "You never actually said."

"You probably don't want to know," Lyrica said, "but he's here for a meeting with a very big Demon."

"Ya know," Sam said as he shook his head, "there was a time I would have thought that was a joke. Then along comes this kid with the whole Council out to get him, and then this kid stands the world on its ear and kicks it a couple of times to see what he can shake out of it. So now that statement doesn't even phase me."

Lyrica's musical laughter brought an automatic smile to my face.

"So who is this great big Demon?"

"His name is Kil'Sin'Deres," I said.

"He's the one you convinced to go back home without fighting last year."

"Yeah," I nodded, "he's different. I have a feeling I'm about to find out how different he is from the rest 'em."

"Let's hope he's a great deal different then."

"Speaking of the meeting," I said, "it's almost time."

"Good luck," Sam said.

"I'll be watching," Lyrica said. "If he tries anything, I'll be there quickly."

I smiled at her, "I don't think he came here for a ruckus. But if he did, he'll get more than he bargained for."

Chapter 10

I had felt the gate open several minutes back, as I walked up the old running trail Lyrica and I had used for years. I didn't rush, even though the bucket full of fried chicken I had brought from the cafeteria smelled delicious.

I entered the clearing where Lyrica had ripped the life out of the area around her. It was starting to come back. Kil'Sin'Deres sat on a rock outcropping.

"Kil'Sin'Deres," I said with a nod.

"Rash'Tor'Ri," he returned my nod. His voice was deep and he spoke clearly.

"I always thought any meeting worth having should be had over food," I said and jumped up on a rock outcropping near him. "I hope you like fried chicken."

I reached into the bucket and pulled out a leg. Then I passed the bucket to him.

He looked at it a moment. I could see surprise rolling through his aura. I could even feel it through the telepathy we shared.

He nodded and took the bucket. Then he reached into the bucket and pulled out a breast. After smelling it, he bit into the meat.

"We have a lizard that tastes much like this when cooked," he said.

I hadn't even been sure they cooked their food. I realized that I knew next to nothing about him or his race. They had been just a ravenous horde to me.

"I hear that a lot," I said. "Most times when someone tries a new food they say it tastes like chicken."

"Yes, we cook our food," he said. "Kresh eat theirs raw. They'll eat anything. Some Kresh'Far as well."

He spoke very good English, to my surprise.

"Why is that?" I asked. "I could tell you were different the first time I met you here."

"It is part of the evolution of my race," he said, "My people are born Kresh. These that your people have referred to as Lesser Demons. They are much like your animals, dogs.

"As we age, and if we survive that stage of our life, we become Kresh'Far. These are more like your people. We become smarter and our minds become stronger.

"Then, if we are lucky enough to survive that stage, we become Kresh'Sor'An. And even fewer become Kresh'Ma'Nar. Fewer still become Kresh'Farrara'Ti. It has taken me two thousand of your years to reach this stage of my existence. Many never go beyond the first two."

"I was born Kresh'Sor'An," he said. "Perhaps this is the reason I am different than most."

"You never went through the first stages," I said.

`He nodded and plucked another piece of chicken from the bucket. He handed the bucket back to me and I pulled out a thigh.

"There are others like me," he said, "I like to believe we are more civilized than our brethren, but we still have that same drive they do for destruction. I fight my drives more than most of my race. I have a stronger drive for something I have only seen in your race."

"What's that?"

"I see your race build things," he said. "You work together to do things one being cannot do alone. This war is my fault. Everything I did, I did for a reason. To bring my race together like yours."

"I failed. My race is even worse now than before I gave them a foe. I let this planet grow far beyond the limits we generally put on a world. I let you advance in technology to the point where my race would have to unite to face it. This Soulguard of yours was unexpected, and I could not stamp it out, I tried."

"And then came you," he said.

"I'm guessing I was a complete surprise," I said.

"Your bloodline is one that was supposed to have been erased long ago", he stated. "It was not supposed to even be a factor in this war. But then you have my blood as well."

"So this would be a perfect way to try to remove me from the picture," I said.

"I believe that removing you would not unite my race," he said. "I have decided that there is only one course of action that has any possibility of uniting my race."

"What would that be?"

"My race must lose this war," he said, "but we are sworn to die before serving the Makers again."

"I've heard this before," I said. "What does that mean? Who are the Makers?"

"Your ancestors were the Makers," he answered.

Everything started to make sense to me. Humans had created the Kresh. That was why their Soulstreams all came through the gates. It was an artificial Source of some sort. That is why the Wraith I had captured said he would never serve the Makers. And that they would eat the Makers. It hadn't really sunk in until this moment.

"That does explain so much," I said, "but how does your race lose and not end up where you are sworn not to go?"

"We must serve one who is neither Kresh nor Human."

"Oh, shit."

I swear, the giant Kresh started laughing, or he was choking on the chicken he just ate.

"Just how in the Hell is that supposed to happen?" I asked.

"I have a plan," he said after his laughter ebbed. "You must Mark us all."

"I'm not that powerful," I said.

"I have been seeing Kresh with a Mark so powerful, it is taking Farrara'Ti. I have made inquiries. They are Marked by Rash'Tor'Ri. I even examined one of these Marks. It was the same that you Lashed out with the last time we were both here. Only it is so much more powerful."

Oh, shit. Gorvelis.

"If you can Mark with such power, we can spread this Mark throughout those such as I. There are more of us. When our numbers are high enough, we can take our world away from those who will not evolve."

"And during this time, they'll be trying to destroy this planet," I stated.

"I cannot stop that," he said with genuine regret in his aura. "They outnumber my kind by massive amounts."

"I see," I said. "What numbers would you bring with your clans?"

"My clans number fourteen million," he said. "With the allies I can bring into this, perhaps another fifteen million. There are hundreds of millions of the others out there. I am certain we can take more, but I must find them."

"Meanwhile, Earth is under attack."

"You must hold, Rash'Tor'Ri," he said. "They will not unify, they will keep attacking but there will be no unity in these attacks. One will try, if he fails, then another. They are limited to one facility, now, so they can only have one Great Gate open at any given time. You must stop them when they come, and I will try to move as quickly as possible on their flanks. They are unable to unify but we are not."

"If possible, kill any Farrara'Ti that comes through. It will set them back for a time and give us more time to build our forces."

"What if you took the facility to Earth?"

"There are Farrara'Ti with as much as ninety million Kresh. They would destroy my clans as if I was not there, and then they would destroy your world as well. We cannot afford to draw that much attention to what is happening here. Not until our numbers are high enough to stand."

"Damn," I said, "there's not really an easy way to do this."

"It is a small chance for any of this to succeed, Rash'Tor'Ri."

"How much attention would you call to yourself if you took the facility of another world? One not openly at war?"

"This is a normal thing. For a larger clan to push out a smaller for one of the colonies."

"The first thing is this," I said. "I can't do that Mark alone. I have to go to Cerres to do that."

"Second, if I go to Cerres, you have to get me back here to face them when they come."

"Third, after this is done, you'll have to take the Cerres facility. This won't be a problem, because the one who holds it is mine. His clans are small and he's a relatively new Farrara'Ti. The world is mine now, and I need it protected. It will also give you a single base of operations to work from."

He had nodded at all these statements.

"And fourth, are you goin' to eat that last piece of chicken?"

As I walked back down off of the mountain range, my mind was still trying to come to grips with what was going on. Everything was spiraling into so much more than I wanted it to be. Before, this war had been pure black and white. It was beginning to turn grey in a lot of areas.

I didn't want to Mark any more people, Kresh or Human, but this may be the only way to end this war without genocide on our part or theirs.

We had talked some details after he handed me the bucket with a single piece of chicken left in it. We would meet again here in Montana in a week. I would either agree to go to another world or I would be turning him down on the offer.

Honestly, I couldn't see any way I could turn down the offer of nearly thirty million Kresh allies, and a possible end to this war before humanity was completely destroyed. If we lost here, it would be just a matter of time before the rest would be exterminated so this couldn't happen again.

I knew we couldn't depend on this plan working, but I feared what was coming. I love the battle and I love killing them. I'm a monster. But I can't be everywhere and people are going to die. A lot of people. The best we can do is prepare as much as we can, and do our best.

Now that Warren is started with the Source Weapons, maybe we can get enough out there to make a difference.

Perhaps we can hold our world long enough to let Kil'Sin'Deres get enough allies.

Perhaps we would push them back far enough to step through that gate in Kansas and take the war to them. With Kil'Sin'Deres on their backs and us on their front. And a new Soulguard built on Cerres hitting their flanks.

Everything boils down to the first step right in front of us.

I must go to another world and use the Shak'Tar as Gorvelis had done. I would have to put everything that all of my clans could do behind that Mark.

Then we would have to see if anything else would go our way.

Chapter 11

"What?!"

"You know," I answered Paige, "you say that a lot."

"Only when you bring this crazy shit to me," she said.

"I can't help it," I said, "I didn't do it."

"Somehow, I know it's your fault."

"It's not always my fault," I protested. "Its Kil'Sin'Deres' fault. He even admitted it."

"You were jealous as soon as we talked about sending someone to another world. I know you set this up, somehow."

"It just makes more sense to send me there than to try to channel that many of the Shak'Tar back here to do this thing."

"Yes, and send our most powerful weapon out where the rest of the Kresh can get to him," said Gregor, who had remained silent so far.

"There are plenty of more powerful..."

"Don't give me that crap about the size of the Soulstream," she interrupted. "When you cut loose, you're probably the most destructive thing on the planet and you know it. We all know it. Yes there are stronger individuals but this is totally different."

"It's true, Colin," Gregor said, "but as I said in the last meeting, 'We need it'. We need allies. We need to face the fact that we may not be victorious here. Humanity needs a back-up plan in the event that we fall. So far we've held them off. But these are just little pushes, according to your contacts."

"That's what I'm sayin', Greg," I said "but, ultimately, this is a Soulguard decision as well as my own. If I go, I'll be taking the seeds to start the Academy on Cerres with me. We were prepared to send our men and women off to do this. How would it look if I refuse to take the same risks that we're asking them to take?"

A long sigh escaped Paige as she sat back in her chair.

"I can't argue that it needs to be done, but it leaves a sour taste in my mouth to trust one of them not to betray you."

"He's risking more on this than I am," I said. "I risk myself and perhaps ten or fifteen others. He is risking his whole clan of fourteen million. He has a great deal more to lose than we do."

"If he was telling the truth," she said.

"My lie detector works on them as well as us," I said, "and he was tellin' the truth."

"What's Lyrica saying about this?"

"She says she's going with me," I said. "I need you to convince her she needs to be here. She doesn't listen when I give the logical reasons why she shouldn't go with me. She might listen to you."

She looked at me for a long moment and with that sour look on her face said, "Asshole."

"What? I can't get her to listen..."

"And I get her to agree to this. Then, you don't make it back. She blames me for that and hates me forever."

"I'll make it back if I have to cut my way through their entire world," I said with some of the rage showing through. "Nothing is goin' to stop me from getting back to her."

"That's what worries me," she said. "This whole thing needs done with finesse. Secrecy is your friend. I'm not sure you even know what the word means. You can't go over there blowing things up."

"I know," I said, "and I'll try to curb my destructive nature long enough to get the mission done."

"OK I'll talk to her," she said, "but I can't guarantee anything."

"That's all I ask."

"And that's plenty," she said.

***

"Looks good, Warren," I said.

We were watching the assembly line in our factory in McMinnville, Tennessee. Everything had started up without trouble. Warren had chosen Tennessee because of some of the benefits that are offered to new companies who start there.

"It's coming along nicely, Sir," he answered.

"I need to talk about some of the paperwork I asked you about."

He nodded and we headed toward on office that was always kept empty for him or me if we were here.

"I'm a little worried," he said as he shut the door. "You've never really worried about any of this before."

"I'm goin' on a trip," I said. "We've been holding the details secret as much as possible. I am going through one of the Gates to sneak onto another world to establish a Soulguard Academy."

He sat back in his chair with an astounded look on his face.

"Really?"

"Yeah," I answered, "and it's a scary prospect but a necessary one. I need the papers official in case anything happens to me. The whole mission is dangerous, to say the least."

"Sounds like it," he said. "The papers are all drawn up. All you have to do is sign them."

"Good, everything to Lyr, right?"

"Yes"

"Excellent," I said, "and did you put the other part I asked for?"

"Yes, sir, but you don't have to do that..."

"Yeah, I do," I said. "None of this would have happened at all without you. You're now a third owner of a weapons company, as is Lyrica. We're goin' to be arms dealers to the world."

"That's not something a person gets to say very often in normal conversation," he said.

"True enough," I said with a laugh, "and that's why I have to say it whenever I can."

"And the last thing I asked about?"

"Yes sir," he said with a grin. "There's a Checkers over in Murfreesboro, which is on the way back to Nashville where the plane is."

"Awesome!"

Chapter 12

As I entered the building where Paige's office was located, I could see Lyrica's Soul through the walls. She was up in Paige's office and her aura was full of turmoil. I sat down in a chair outside to wait until the fireworks were over.

"I can't let him go alone," I heard Lyrica, "because you know he'll do something stupid."

"I know what you're saying, Lyr," Paige answered, "but what happens if they come while he's over there? Can the world afford to have both of its primary weapons off world at the same time?

"I can't order you not to go. You've never officially joined the Soulguard, and I understand why better than most. But this is bigger than you, and it's bigger than me."

"And what if they get him?"

"Then you and I will walk through one of those damn gates, and we'll rip their world in two."

"You promise that to me and I will risk it," Lyrica said fiercely. "Because, if he doesn't make it back, I'm going after him and God help anyone or anything that gets in my way."

"And I'll be right there with you, Honey," Paige said. "I swear it to you right now."

As Lyrica exited Paige's office, I met her with an embrace.

"I love you, my Little Angel," I said softly, "and there is nothing on this world or the next that could keep me from coming back to you."

"And I love you, my Angel," she said, "but you'd better come back or they have to deal with me. You just blow shit up, but I'll tear their world apart."

"Now I have to go to work," she said, "We'll talk later."

She walked out the front of the building, her aura still in turmoil. I hate that I'm the one who is causing the turmoil in her Soul. But we can't risk both of us, and she can't do the Mark I need to do. So I have to be the one who goes.

If it was the other way around, I would feel the same as she does. I don't know if I could do as she is. It's a stronger person who can take that high road and think of the world before themselves. She is doing that, I'm not sure if I could.

I walked into Paige's office and she was looking at me with distaste.

"I'm sorry," I said. "You're the only person she might have listened to."

"That may be true," she said, "but it doesn't mean I have to like it."

"True enough."

***

I met the others, who would be going across to Cerres to build the new academy, in Montana. Kil'Sin'Deres would be meeting us the next day to escort us through the Gate and onto another world.

I was excited as I could be. I'd read science fiction all of my life, and this was one of the dreams of any Sci-Fi fan. To actually walk on another planet.

"Sam," I said to the first team member I met, "glad you decided to do this."

Sam Keller would be the head of the Soulguard forces that would be built on Cerres. He would head up any militant action taken by this Soulguard.

"It's goin' to be interesting," he said, "to say the least."

"Darrel," I said to the next in the team, "I'm certainly glad you joined as well."

He nodded. I could see the fear of me roiling through his aura. Paige and Gregor had taken the effects of supporting me in stride, but Darrel had been traumatized by having his Soulstream ripped open and doubled in size.

Darrel would be the Dean of the Mage Academy on Cerres. It would be his job to find people with the Soulstreams large enough to Pull the Source. He would train them to use that power before it killed them. In the meantime, he would run the day to day part of keeping something like this going.

There were ten Mages of varied strengths going along with them and twenty Guards. I recognized most of them but there were several I hadn't met before.

"Any weapons," I said, "will need to be concealed. We are under the guise of a group of humans taken by Kil'Sin'Deres and his bunch.

Everyone will be provided for after we get there so there's not much we'll need to take with us. Any personal effects need to be hidden as well. When Humans are captured they are stripped of these things. Jewelry, pictures, things like that. So keep 'em hidden."

"This group is the biggest we can risk sending at a time, and there will be others slipped through over the next few months. The Soulguard thanks you, and I thank you. So get ready and we'll set out tomorrow to make history."

***

The quarters Lyrica and I shared at the Academy were much larger than the ones I had used when I was here before. I think they were the quarters of a Councilor.

Lyrica lounged in a huge bath tub.

"That was Khalib down there," she said.

"Yeah," I said, "he's got more experience than most in infiltration. He's a good choice for the team."

"And his family is left behind," she said.

"Temporarily, my love," I said. "He wouldn't take them until he's seen it's safe enough to move through the gates."

"I wish you didn't have to do this," she said. "It's not fair that you have to always be the one."

"Me too, honey," I said, "but the fact is, I'm the only one who can do this and we need allies.

With this one move, we can change the whole course of the war to come."

"Before, all we had to look forward to was an endless supply of Kresh, coming through the Gates to kill us. I've shown you the memories from my Shak'Tar. You've seen them. They have the numbers to just swamp us if the right clan goes after us.

"But, this," I said, "this could actually win the war, given enough time."

"All true," she said, "but I still wish I could just have you to myself. I don't want to share you with the world. I damn sure don't want to share you with fourteen other worlds, too."

"Until tomorrow, though," she said, "you are all mine. So you better come join me."

"That I can do."

Chapter 13

I couldn't hide my excitement as our group approached the gate.

"I used to equate the feeling I get near one of these with evil," I said to the giant walking beside me. "It has the same sort of power source as the one that is connected to your Soulstream."

"Soulstream is not a new word to me," He said in his deep rumbling voice. "We never knew we were tethered to our own world until you closed a gate and killed a whole clan by cutting this Soulstream."

"You never went through a gate and shut it behind you?" I asked.

"We could not open one from this side," he said. "When we open a gate and walk through, it stays open until we come back. After the second attack, we knew the tether would move to another gate if one was open. So now we can turn off the great gates when the horde has passed through it."

Our group was surrounded by Wraiths and Soldiers as we approached the open gate. I could see the nervousness of the others, so I moved forward to the front of the group.

"All right," I said, "here goes."

Kil'Sin'Deres moved up beside me, and I followed him into the vortex of power that made up the portal.

I expected something like what I had seen in movies as the lights would stretch, but I guess the movies hadn't really gotten that right.

It was instant. My eyes saw the purple and black energy one second and, as they passed the edge of it, the sight changed to a raised platform in a large room.

"Holy shit!"

My whole body tingled, and I felt the Source stutter and change. It was a subtle difference but I could sense much more power down inside the planet than I could feel inside earth.

I stepped forward so that the next in line wouldn't run into me.

"I will hide your mind glow, Rash'Tor'Ri," Kil'Sin'Deres said. "From here until we reach Cerres, you must not use any form of Lash. I cannot hide it if you are using it actively."

"Ok," I said. "I'm not really planning to use that particular skill except to do the Mark for you."

"You are an odd being, Rash'Tor'Ri," he said. "My race begins using the Lash the moment they evolve enough to use it. Why would you handicap yourself by only using half of your birthright?"

On some level, he was right. I had paid in blood for the skills that my birth had granted me. But the use of that Lash was just the opposite of the freedom I wanted to bring to the people of these other worlds.

It was too late to do anything about the people on Cerres except try to provide some sort of defense.

"Yeah, I hear that a lot."

The giant chuckled.

I could feel the Kresh outside of the room. There were more than I had ever felt before. I knew the others would be feeling that same presence I could feel. It was a bit overwhelming. We waited until the whole group had stepped through the gate. Then the gate was gone.

"Guess there's no way to go but forward," Keller said with a grin.

"It would help if your people looked fearful, as most humans who come through these gates. They look like they are ready to invade and conquer."

"All right guys, put on your scared faces and get into position, in case everything goes to shit."

"Terry," Sam said to one of the Mages, "you and I are supports for the boss. Barnes get ready with a shield in case we need it. You're the strongest one here. Mages to the center, Guards around the outside."

"Now they really look like they want to invade," Kil'Sin'Deres said.

"Give it a minute," I said, "and they'll get settled."

Once everyone was positioned, they stepped one step in different directions. The organization disappeared, and we looked like a mob of humans again.

"If all goes right," I said, "we won't be needin' to do any fightin'. But we're ready if we do."

Kil'Sin'Deres nodded and we headed for the opposite end of the big room.

When the door opened and we stepped outside, the light seemed just a little off kilter.

"Different type of star," Darrel said softly, "different light."

"Makes sense," I said.

I'd been in big cities a few times. New York and Chicago were large cities, but they had nothing on what I was looking at in front of us. The buildings were huge and stretched far into the sky.

The doors were lower than would be comfortably for the height of a Kresh. They were human-sized doors. That would mean they were made by the Makers. And that would mean they were thousands of years old.

The streets were packed with Kresh and Humans. Most of the Humans kept their eyes downcast. They wore various home-made garments. There were a few in jeans scattered amongst the crowds.

Having all of the Kresh around me was bringing that monster inside me close to the surface. As I saw the enslaved humans, it was clawing at the walls of my mind.

"Rash'Tor'Ri, you must calm your mind," Kil'Sin'Deres said. "There is nothing we can do yet for these people. There will come a time."

I tore my eyes from the groups of slaves and followed Kil'Sin'Deres through the throngs of Kresh.

That was, perhaps the hardest five miles I had ever walked. The whole way, I had to keep the beast locked down.

That all changed the second we entered the Cerres facility. Every eye within sight of us turned to me immediately, and I felt like I had walked into my own home.

A Farrara'Ti walked toward us. I knew his name was Pos'Far'Nadir, and I had seen him in a memory. He was the Kresh'Farrara'Ti that Gorvelis had marked on Cerres.

"Rash'Tor'Ri," he said in a raspy voice, "you have come to Cerres?"

"You might say, I'm passing through, Pos'Far'Nadir," I said. "These are allies. After what we do on Cerres, they will be coming to join you in holding the Cerres facility."

Pos'Far'Nadir nodded and led the way inside the facility. In the center of the facility was a large clearing with a huge assembly in the center. It was a massive ring that looked like something out of a TV series I used to watch called Stargate. It was the size of one of the Great Gates that open onto Earth.

As the Gate began to charge up, I watched the power it pulled. It came from the Source!

The Makers had created something that could Pull its power from the Source of all life and use that power to open a hole in space to another world.

"It's powered by the Source," I said.

"The Source?" Sam asked.

"Yeah, it draws its power from the Source. I have no idea how it uses that to do what it does. But it's connected to the Source."

"You may be onto something with those Source Weapons then," Sam said. "I bet there's something similar inside this."

"Have you noticed how everything in this city that we've seen is too small for the Kresh?" Darrel asked.

"It was created by the Makers," Kil'Sin'Deres answered. "They were as you are. Small."

I chuckled. I was feeling so much more at ease since I had entered. The Mark had made these Kresh my family, just as much as it had the Romanians I had marked. There was a whole planet of people who would feel this way. Maybe the Mark wasn't all bad.

The rage that had been pounding at my mind's walls began to ease off.

This could be a wonderful thing for me, personally, but do I have the right to use this again on people? And where do I draw the line between people of my race and people of the Kresh. Do I have the right to do this Mark on Kil'Sin'Deres? It is his request, but is it right?

The Gate flared to life and the portal hummed with power. I couldn't feel it like I could feel when someone Pulls from the Source. But I could see the power flow into the machinery and the tendrils of power twirl and reach out to another world.

Pos'Far'Nadir motioned for me to proceed.

I stepped forward onto the third planet I had set foot on in a single day. How often does a person get to say that?

Chapter 14

Just like when I stepped into the facility, it felt like I was home. The second I stepped through the gate, every head turned toward me.

"I can feel them," I said. "I can feel them all."

Sam had been right behind me.

"All of who?"

"All the people, Sam. I can feel all the people on this world."

"But there are millions," he said.

"They're everywhere," I said, "and I'm having trouble concentrating."

"You must push this to the back of your mind, Rash'Tor'Ri," Kil'Sin'Deres said. "This is what it means to be Farrara'Ti. You will feel every being you Mark."

I pushed the awareness to the back of my mind. I had done something similar back when I was a child. I had made it where I could turn my Sight off and on. Otherwise I would always be seeing power flows instead of what a regular person sees. Now I did so again with this awareness of all those around me. I couldn't shut it off but I could reduce it to a sort of background noise.

"There," I said, "maybe that'll do it."

A group of people were walking across the clearing toward us. The person in the lead was Touran Gorvelis, and his Soul was in turmoil.

He strode forward and knelt before me.

"I have failed you, Master," he said. "And I offer you my life in return."

I grasped his shoulder and pulled him to his feet.

"You haven't failed me, Touran," I said. "We have such different backgrounds, how could you have known?"

"But..."

"We're good, Touran. Just no more Marks on Humans. We are now responsible for the safety of this world and that will, for the most part, fall on you. I am here but for a short time. And then you'll have to take care of this place when I go back."

"Why are you here?" he asked. "I thought you wouldn't leave until your world was safe."

I started to answer but I just did what they all do. I just gave him a mental information dump.

"I see," he said as he looked at Kil'Sin'Deres. "I have never seen a Kresh who would willingly take the Mark. Much less a Farrara'Ti as powerful as Kil'Sin'Deres."

"It's just part of a much larger plan," I said.

"I see that, as well. It just might work."

"This half silent-half voice conversation is messin' with my Chi," Sam said. "Some of us ain't telepathic. You're freakin' us out here."

"He will be a joy to work with," Gorvelis said. "Are you sure he is not Marked? He has your attitude."

"Nope, ya can't blame his attitude on me. That's all his."

"I'm standin' right here," Sam said

"I'm not so certain," Gorvelis said. "He feels a lot like you."

"Right here," Sam said again.

I laughed, "Touran Gorvelis, this is Sam Keller and Darrel Barnes. They will be setting up a Soulguard Academy here on Cerres. Sam will be the one in charge of the military side of it and Darrel the academic side. The others will be trainers and instructors."

Gorvelis was grinning.

"This is a step on the path of defending Cerres. You've seen the next step in my mind."

"It will take a week to get the Shak'Tar back here for the Mark. Do you have that much time?" Gorvelis asked.

"Probably not," I said, "How many do you have here?"

"Perhaps a hundred," he said

"It'll do," I said, "and I'll use the Kresh from the facility."

"Kresh do not do that sort of thing," he said.

I looked at Kil'Sin'Deres and he was grinning.

"My Kresh will," I said.

He looked into my burning eyes and said, "They may do it, indeed."

"They will," I said, "and it'll be the key to winning the war."

He was still doubtful but I was certain it would work. If not, well, I guess I would wait a week.

"Send for Pos'Far'Nadir and all of his Ma'Nar," I said, "It shouldn't take long to set this up, so we'll do it tomorrow. In the meantime, what is there to eat on this planet? I can't go back without trying the food out."

"Always thinkin' with his stomach," I heard Sam mutter.

"We will have a feast!" Gorvelis shouted, and the people in the clearing were all back in motion.

"What did he just say?" Sam asked.

I hadn't even noticed Gorvelis' switch back to the native language of Cerres. The advantage of telepathy, I suppose.

"He said we are going to have a feast."

"It figures."

"Let us get your men settled," Gorvelis said, "There are plenty of quarters here. This is the Capitol of Cerres and houses well over a thousand people."

"Good," I said, "Cause there are goin' to be a lot more here, soon. We'll be filtering more through the gates as quickly as we can and I plan for the Shak'Tar to be in training as soon as possible."

"As you wish, Master," he said with a grin.

"You don't have to call me master."

"I know."

***

The facility on this side of the gate was as technologically advanced as the other side. I was to find that the rest of this world was much less so. Cerres had been held back from advancing like Earth had done. They were at a level about with what Earth had been in the seventeen hundreds.

For decades, any people who advanced past that stage were removed be the Kresh. If this had been done on Earth, our war would have been impossible.

"You deliberately let us progress so you would have an enemy," I said to Kil'Sin'Deres. "I see where you were going with it. If things work like I plan tomorrow, you'll see if your people will unify for something."

"What you will ask of them, no Kresh would even think to ask," he said. "I never would even think to ask my people to do a thing like this. That is why I came to you. With my Mark, my people would just look at me in confusion if I asked them for this."

"Let's hope we get a better reaction than that," I said.

"I sent for the Ma'Nar of your clans to come here and join this Mark as well," said Kil'Sin'Deres.

I hadn't even thought of that. That would give us four more to add to the power level. One Kresh'Ma'Nar would equal quite a few of the Shak'Tar, and a Farrara'Ti would make a massive difference.

"They say my strength is the level of a Farrara'Ti. Add another one and eighteen Ma'Nar, plus a hundred or so Shak'Tar and we should get quite a Mark," I said as I figured in my head.

"That is so," Kil'Sin'Deres said, "If they will understand and accept what you ask of them. It will change our Race completely, if we succeed with this plan."

"Are you sure this is what you want?" I asked. "You know what the Mark does. It changes you. Do you want to take the risk of changing?"

"I must," he said, "for the sake of my people."

"I don't want to rule the world, Kil'Sin'Deres. Part of me longs for peace, another for the war. What if my Mark brings you no peace? What if you are at war with yourself all the time? What if the cure is worse than the disease?"

He laughed, "Rash'Tor'Ri, I have been at war with myself for two thousand years. Some of my choices have been losses, some have been victories. The key to fighting this battle inside me is to keep making choices. When you are afraid to choose, you have lost the war."

"That makes more sense than I would like to admit," I said.

"I am not searching for peace, Rash'Tor'Ri," he said. "I search for the unity of my race. Whether it be in war or peace. I tried to unite my race in war with yours. I failed. Now I will try to unite my race in peace with yours. It will result in war with parts of my own race, but I can see a chance of unity amongst many of the others.

"My race will never unify if not under a Mark. We would never even understand what you call freedom. The Mark gives us what structure my race has. Without it, utter chaos."

He had made my decision for me, it seemed. I would Mark Kil'Sin'Deres on the next day, for better or worse. Choices must be made or you have already lost the war within yourself. It was sad that I needed to take life lessons from a Demon, but I had more in common with Kil'Sin'Deres than I did with most Humans.

Chapter 15

"Feast," I said, "means much more than it did before today."

"No doubt," said Vivian Kray.

Vivian was one of the Mages who had come over with us.

"I love food," I said, "but I don't think I could even sample all the different things they have laid out here."

"I bet you'll try," said Sam with a laugh as he walked up.

"Of course," I said.

"Never doubted ya, Boss."

There were at least ten different animals that had been roasted. Various vegetables and a dark colored bread on the huge table.

There were Shak'Tar and Kresh and regular Humans all throughout the enormous room. The tables were of wood and it clashed in my mind with the metallic walls of the building.

The Makers had made things to last thousands of years. But there was nothing added to what they left. The Kresh aren't technological beings and they had just used what was there. I would have guessed that the Gates, if studied, would advance Earth's technology at a pace that would be staggering.

And now, Cerres would advance as well. We would bring this world into the same level of technology that Earth has reached.

It would take some time, I was certain. But, if all went right, we would have enough time to send some experts over to examine the tech left by the Makers. It would be very high on my list of things to do when I returned to Earth.

"Look at this room," Gorvelis said. "Can you see the hope of peace, here? I can."

He was right, three races of beings sat together around a table of food.

"I can see it, Touran," I said, "and it gives me hope that we can survive all of this and coexist."

"I know now that you don't want the Mark used, Master," he said, "but it is not all bad. The inhabitants of Cerres spent the majority of their time killing one another in useless wars for many purposes. All with the terrible cloud of the Kresh looming over their heads. A waste of life."

"There is peace among them all now. They are of a single clan. They are all a family. This is what the Mark can be. With the Kresh, the Mark is to mark possession. This Mark is different, it Marks... the word escapes me in your tongue. We belong together."

"I can see the beauty of it, Touran," I said, "I really can. When I stepped onto this planet I felt like I had come home. But it isn't freedom. Freedom is the right to choose."

"You once told me that you could choose not to follow a Mark, but I don't see anyone choosing not to. At least some of the Shak'Tar would have chosen not to. Humans are both good and evil. There would have been some of the ones who relished evil that would have chosen not to follow.

"I see Souls, I see the changes that my Mark made in both the Human and the Kresh. It changes people, Touran. They choose to follow because they were changed into people who would choose to follow. You understand?"

"I think I do," he answered, "but you are about to use the Mark again tomorrow."

"The difference is that Kil'Sin'Deres came to me and asked for this. He chose the path and that is what freedom stands for.

"America is a free country," I said, "Yet, if you look at it, people don't seem to be free. They're controlled by a government. The key to that system is that Americans choose their government. It's not perfect and over the years the dream has been corrupted some. But the choice was and is there."

"This is much cleaner than the freedom you speak of," he said, motioning out toward the world of Cerres.

"But this has to be a choice, too," I said. "If a person chooses to join this, it's different than if that choice was placed on them. I chose the fate of you and your men the day I Marked you. You didn't choose it. I did. I didn't have a clue what I was doing at the time, but it's still on me."

He nodded slowly and I could see and feel his emotions roiling.

"And I chose to do this," he said. "This world's fate is on me."

"Yes, it's on both of us," I said. "For you, Touran, the war is over. Your sole job is to care for these people. Protect them, help them. You are responsible for them, as am I. I am placing you in the position of Governor of Cerres. Keep this world safe. Be ready for more people to come."

He wasn't happy to be removed from the war. He'd been aching to kill the Kresh from the moment they destroyed his love. But I could also see and feel the iron resolve that had carried him through years of servitude to the very beings he hated. That resolve would make a great leader of the man.

"I will do as you say," He said, "and if any of these people wish to join our ranks?"

"If they come and ask to be Marked, you tell them exactly what will happen. If they choose to do it, do as you see fit. They must choose of their own free will."

"It will be done."

"Don't think of it as a punishment, Touran," I said. "This position is vital. You'll build a sanctuary for Humanity. And you'll be creating an army with the Soulguard Academy here. When all is ready, we'll be attacking the Kresh from two different directions."

"I see the need for this, Rash'Tor'Ri," he said, "but I will miss the action of my former life."

"I understand, completely," I said. "When the war we fight is over, I'll face much the same thing. When it's done, I'll come and join you, here, with our family."

"You are certain you will win this war?"

"Absolutely," I said. "Just look around you Touran. Three races about to have dinner together. Where else have you seen anything like this? How can we lose when we can see this already happening?

"I used to only want to kill 'em after what happened to my parents, and after what happened when they came for me. All I saw was an evil, hate-filled horde. Thanks to you, I see others that are different. Now I don't have an unreasoning hatred for all Kresh. Just the majority of 'em.

"And I guess that's a fair enough start."

"You are an odd being, Rash'Tor'Ri," Gorvelis said, "I never had that unreasoning hate of all Kresh. I hated the ones who killed her. I hated the one who was our Master. But there were others that were different. I knew this long ago. That is why we lured Pos'Far'Nadir to that meeting where we Marked him. He is different. He accepted the Mark, unlike our Master, Sol'Kor'Vanas.

"You may find more than you think you will when you start looking for the ones willing to change. The Kresh have not changed in thousands of years. Perhaps many of them truly want to."

"Let's hope so," I said, "My world is depending on it. Thank God they don't have two of the Gate facilities to my world any more. We might have a chance with only one Great Gate at a time. Two at a time would roll us under in sheer numbers."

"Pelin has reported that it was your ancestor that did that. Is this true?"

"By my understanding, it is."

"I wish it wasn't so dangerous over here for you," he said, "You should see what was left of that facility. It was a building just as large as the one for Cerres. There is nothing left but a great hole in the ground that swallowed the whole building and several of the unimportant buildings surrounding it."

"That would be a sight to see," I said, "How far away from the Cerres gate is it?"

"Twenty or so of your miles," he said, "Much too far to risk traveling amidst the Kresh with your mind glow."

"Twenty miles and it's still inside the city?"

"Hub is very large, Rash'Tor'Ri," he said. "It takes days to walk from one end to the other."

"All that technology, and there's no fast transit system?" I asked.

He took a moment to put the term together with the image I was seeing in my mind.

"The Makers may have had some sort of system. I have never seen or heard of it. Kresh just use what technology is left. They kept some Humans to throw into the machines to make them work. The Gates require a Human to open them. They kept colonies of Humans just for that purpose and killed and ate many to keep the others in line."

"I think I understand why the gates need Humans," I said. "I made some weapons under much the same principles."

His mouth dropped open as he saw in my mind the Source weapon in use.

"Can any Human use these weapons?"

"As far as I know," I said. "Why?"

"Only one in four can use the machines," he said, "They tend to kill the ones they put in the machines that fail."

That sounded a little ominous. We hadn't tried anyone except John on the guns, so far. If we were limited as the humans on this side were, it could be a problem.

"We haven't tested enough to know if our odds run the same," I said. "I hope it isn't, but the Makers were so far advanced past us that I'm expecting worse, now. Thanks, Touran, way to ruin a guy's day."

"Always willing to help, Rash'Tor'Ri."

Damn, even the Shak'Tar were smart asses. What was the world coming to?

Gorvelis laughed.

Damn telepathy.

He laughed even harder.

Chapter 16

"Apparently," I said, "whatever this metal the Makers created can stand up to the Source flowing through it without degrading."

"That's interesting," Darrel said, looking closer at the walls of the building built around the spot where the Great Gate opened. "It would make for a much better material for the Source Weapons."

"I wish we knew what it was," I said. "I should try to cut a piece of it and take it back with me."

"Definitely," he said.

This was the most I had spoken with Darrel Barnes since First Kansas, and I found that I missed talking with my friend. He and Paige had been my friends at the Academy. We had gone our separate ways but had kept in touch. Until I ripped his Soulstream wide open and left him unconscious from too much of the Source flowing through him.

I had made many mistakes that day. Mistakes that I would change if I could. I had healed my mom, but something in her abdomen, where the huge cut had been, hadn't been in the right place when I did it. She was still strong and fast but her movements were limited after that.

I had tied myself to the Source with huge tendrils of power to finish cutting the huge Source cables that held that gate open. Behind me were two hundred new Mages who could have supported me, and I didn't realize. I spent a week or so in a Source

Coma for that one. I would have died without my friends supporting me, and Lyrica traipsing through my head to bring me back.

I lost men when they lost focus and the Source burned them up. Friends who died because I didn't know what I was doing. Pat Shoffner had been a good kid. He was one of those who hadn't held focus well enough.

I'd learned a lot since then. Brute force isn't always the answer. Since the machine is powered by the Source, perhaps I could manipulate the Gates in some way. Maybe, after this war is over, if I survive it, I can experiment on one to find out.

"Maybe we can find an out of the way spot, and see if you can cut it," he said.

We headed around the building to a spot on the back side. I had crafted a smaller version of the cutter I had used in Kansas some time back while experimenting. This one would focus a six inch feeder down to a quarter of an inch and it would burn hotter than a plasma torch.

I Pulled and sent it into that six inch feeder. The quarter inch cutter glowed white as it fired. I couldn't actually see if it was cutting because I needed a welding helmet. But I ran the beam around in a square.

When I shut it off, Darrel looked closer.

"Son of a bitch," he said, "That barely scratched it."

He was right. I could see where my cutter had ran around the square, but the cut was hardly even there. How the hell had Merlin destroyed a whole building made of this stuff?

I heard people running around the building.

"What the hell is goin' on?" Sam asked, looking for the enemy. They had felt my Pull and come running.

Gorvelis was right behind Sam.

"I wanted a sample of this metal to take back with me," I said. "I was trying to cut a piece out of the wall. It doesn't cut very easy."

"No need for desecrating our Capitol building, Rash'Tor'Ri," Gorvelis said. "There are many small scraps of this metal. I will send some with you."

"I guess I should've asked," I said. "Sorry of I desecrated something, I didn't think."

"You didn't," he said with a chuckle. "I was being, what did you call it? A smart ass?"

"I go to another friggin' world, and I still get the same shit."

"Maybe ya shoulda thought of that before you put a Mark of your smart assed self into the minds of a bunch of telepathic assassins," Sam shrugged, "Just sayin'".

"What's your damn excuse?"

"Oh, I'm just a smart ass, by nature."

"I see," I said, "I'm just surrounded by smartasses."

"It seems so."

***

I stood in the center of the clearing in front of the Gate that Pos'Far'Nadir had just come through with eighteen Kresh'Ma'Nar. Among them were my four Ma'Nar.

"Welcome Dun'Fil'Resaf, Pas'Lod'Tores, Sin'Kol'Wari, Jor'Som'Marak," I greeted my four Ma'Nar, "Are you ready to make history?"

"It worries me when Rash'Tor'Ri wants to make history," Dun'Fil'Resaf said. "It is never a small thing with you. What is it you wish from your Ma'Nar?"

Parts of what Dun'Fil'Resaf said was in English and other parts in Kresh. I had no trouble understanding them since my telepathic link with them was so strong. My bond with those I Mark is much stronger than the telepathic connection I can form with anyone else.

"Here's what I'm gonna want," I said, "and this goes for all of you. When I give the word, you all will focus on the Mark inside you and, just as you would Mark another, you Lash that Mark at me."

"It is your Mark, Rash'Tor'Ri, it will do nothing."

"I intend to show you that it will do something," I said, "something you have never even imagined."

"We will do as you say, Rash'Tor'Ri," Pos'Far'Nadir said.

Dun'Fil'Resaf nodded, as did the rest of the Kresh arrayed before me. There were a hundred and fifty Shak'Tar, which was a better number than I had expected. It had just worked out that a group had been on their way through Hub and slipped through to join us.

I was a little nervous. I'd seen Gorvelis do this in a memory of one of his scouts. He had used the combined power of five hundred Shak'Tar to Mark Pos'Far'Nadir. It was a powerful Mark but four of the Ma'Nar standing here could make one that powerful if combined.

The mental strength of what I had standing before me was staggering in comparison.

What if I failed?

"You are Rash'Tor'Ri," Kil'Sin'Deres said from behind me. "Your men say you don't even know how to fail."

"I'm glad they have all that faith in me, 'cause this is a pretty big move."

"But look around you, Rash'Tor'Ri, at what has been accomplished already," he said, "from a single Mark."

"Most fight the Mark," he said. "Worry not, I have no intention of fighting. I welcome it."

"All right," I said and turned to face Kil'Sin'Deres. "Are you ready?"

He nodded.

I raised my hand in the air and focused my will on the Mark. In essence, it was everything that made me who I am. The loyalty I had learned from Kharl and Kyra, the honor I had learned throughout my years serving with the brave men and women in the Soulguard. The hope I held for the end of a war that had already consumed much and would consume much more. My losses of friends and family, and the gaining of more of them. My love that centered around the woman that I adore. My hate of all that stood in our path. My fears, my dreams, and my bottomless pit of rage.

All of this, I focused and yelled, "Now!"

The wall of mental strength hit me, and it was all that I had brought forward. I landed on my knees as it hit me like a physical blow. Then I added all of my will, and Lashed forward at the lone figure standing before me.

I saw his Soul as the Lash hit him and he staggered backwards to stumble and fall. It was as if parts of his Soul were obliterated in the massive wave of mental power that washed over him.

Then it was done, and I staggered forward toward my new brother. I could feel his mind as he was studying the Mark. I could see the surprise at the changes he felt inside himself.

"You ok?"

"That was different," he said as he sat back up from the prone position he had landed in.

"But are you still you?" I asked.

"Oh yes," he answered, "and much more, now."

"Good," I said and turned back to see the utter astonishment rolling through the Souls of the Kresh that had been a part of the Mark.

The Shak'Tar had known what to expect but they had no idea of the scale of power that would be used. They had done the single group Mark. This had been hundreds of times more powerful.

"History," I said as I walked past a stunned Dun'Fil'Resaf.

He just nodded.

Chapter 17

"It was a good thing you sent all of your Soulguard friends back across to Hub before you did the Mark," Gorvelis said, "That powerful of a Lash would have Marked everything within ten of your miles."

"It might have been a little overkill," I said.

"No," he said, "for what Kil'Sin'Deres plans, he will need that powerful of a Mark. He plans to Mark other Farrara'Ti with it."

"I must use the Mark sparingly," Kil'Sin'Deres said from behind us. "Used in the right places, we can build our clan large enough to rival the largest of clans. We must be large enough to defeat the largest of clans without so many losses that we cannot face the next one."

"I can see that."

"If I Mark the Farrara'Ti, we gain his clans. If I were to try to Mark all who I see the Mark would lose its potency."

"So, it takes some time to accomplish," I said. "I can understand that. In the meantime, build forces here and in the Cerres facility. Keep this place safe and we keep the others busy trying to kill us on Earth. I know it's the best plan we can come up with right now, but I wish it could be something that doesn't cost so many lives."

"There is something I wish to speak to you about," Gorvelis said. "We have heard rumors of someone who calls himself the Prophet of Rash'Tor'Ri. He is moving from village to village on Kresh. Where he goes, the villages are abandoned. They say he has killed Kresh in defense of humans and he talks of freedom."

"I like him already," I said. "Does anyone know who he is or where he came from?"

"I have sent agents to find him and report back with what they learn. One agent is to report here, the other to report to you, personally. I am of a mind to help this Prophet, but I will await your orders on this one."

"It all depends on where these people are disappearing to," I said. "If it's some trick, and these folks are bein' hurt then we stop him. If he is real and he's hiding people, we should tell him of a certain place I know where he could hide millions of people."

"I agree," Gorvelis said. "If he is real, we will help. There is much room on Cerres."

"From what I understand, there's a lot of room in Hub to hide people. All those buildings and no one uses any of the upper floors."

"True," he said, "we used one of the buildings at one point to gather all of the Shak'Tar. There is room to hide thousands up in those buildings. The Kresh are uncomfortable in the small spaces that were designed for the Makers. They just keep them blocked off and use the lower floors that are designed to house the Gates."

"Is the Cerres facility the same?"

"Yes."

"If you don't mind the cramped spaces, Kil'Sin'Deres, I'd like to look at the upper floors on the way back."

"I can stand them, Rash'Tor'Ri," he said. "I have been in worse places than that on your world. All of the caverns were the price I paid to bring my plan to fruition. As it happens, it came by a different set of actions. At least it has come. What I saw yesterday tells me that this plan will work. You taught those who would never have believed how to unify."

"We have Gorvelis and his men to thank for that one," I said. "It had never even occurred to me until I saw what they did here."

There was another of the Shak'Tar over on the other side of the room. He was in conversation with one of the Soulguards that had come across with us. David Mitchell was explaining how to tie the Soulstream into the knotted stream of a Guard.

I could already see the Shak'Tar, Sain Kifert's, Soulstream twitching as he was listening to Mitchell.

Mitchell motioned like he was looping around and the Shak'Tar followed with his mind. I saw the Stream bend and loop around, and his aura blazed in surprise and awe as the first step, which was the hardest for most, was completed.

David slapped him on the back with a huge grin.

"I knew telepathic recruits would progress fast, but damn."

Gorvelis looked over and his eyes widened as he read in Sain's mind what had just happened.

"That will be quite useful," he said.

"It's been quite useful on my world, Touran," I said with a grin.

"Are you ready to return to Earth, Rash'Tor'Ri?" Kil'Sin'Deres asked.

"Yeah," I said, "I guess so. I need to talk to Sam before we go. I want him to come take a look at the upper floors of the Cerres building. I have some ideas."

"I will be ready at the gate."

"I'll be there in a few minutes," I said and went on the search for Sam Keller.

It didn't take long to find him. He was talking to Golin Frey, one of Gorvelis' scouts.

"Hey, Sam," I said, "I'm about to head back and I wanted you to join me for a minute, if you have time."

"I'll get back with ya on this, Golin," he said and turned to me. "What ya got in mind?"

"On our way out, we're goin' to look into the upper floors of the Cerres building. I'm thinkin it would be a good place to use as a posting for the new Guards as they get through training. They say there's room for thousands up in the tops of these buildings. Seems like a waste of space that we could be usin'."

"Now, that's a good idea," he said. "I heard one of the scouts say the Kresh don't use anything above the lower floors 'cause of the cramped spaces.

We can take care of that for ya, though. I'm sure Lyrica is pacin' the floor the longer you're here."

"You do have a point," I said. "As soon as you get a report ready, send it. We also need to know when it's safe to send another group of Guards through, as well as family members. The Shak'Tar seem to be able to move around, even when the wars are goin' on."

"Will do, Boss," he said. "Now get back home and get ready for the bastards to poke their heads back out."

"Sure thing, and good luck over here."

"Same to you. I think you need it more than I do. There are about twenty million Kresh between us and them after Kil'Sin'Deres gets his people in place."

"True enough."

I turned and headed toward the Gate. I met Touran who carried a satchel.

"Your metal samples," he said.

"Good deal," I said. "If we can figure this stuff out we can use it for the guns."

"Is it so strong, that it can't be cut?"

"No, I can cut it with more power. It's just stronger than the hardened steel we've been usin'. A plasma torch could cut it, given enough time."

"I hope it is useful."

"Me too, Touran," I said and shook his hand. "You've done an incredible thing here."

"Thank you," he said. "I actually expected to see more anger after the information that was sent to me."

"In all honesty, I was angry. But I've learned some since then about the world you, and all of these people were raised in. You did what comes natural to you, and I can't really fault you for that. It helps that, the second I stepped onto this world, I felt at peace. Like I had come home."

"It is the way of the Mark."

"I know it's selfish of me to want something like this," I said, "but part of me longs for peace. The other part wants to rip everything apart. Here, I don't feel them warring with each other. Does that make any sense to you?"

"We have the Blood in us, Rash'Tor'Ri," he said, "but the things you can do have brought you more changes than come to us. You can touch their Source as well as your own. It makes you strong, but it feeds the Blood inside. You must be careful and avoid this if you wish to remain who you are. I once told you to embrace that which is inside you. I'm glad that you refused. I think, in your case, it would have been the wrong thing to do."

"The peace you feel here is real, and we would welcome you with open arms," he said. "But if you came here now, it would be a temporary peace at best. They would finish your world and come for us next. You have charged me to end my war and govern these people. I charge you to fight that war until you can come and take my place. Make the protection of these people something that is not needed any more. Then you can come home and be at peace."

My eyes burned as his words sank in. I couldn't say no to what he was saying. It's what I was born for. I was born to fight this fight.

But I could also see a glimmer of a hope that I could live after the war. I always worry about the monster I have inside me. About what I would be if I didn't have the Kresh to fight. Thanks to Gorvelis and his people, I know there is a place that I can go when it is all over and be at peace.

"I swear it, Touran," I said. "I'll fight the war. You keep this place safe. When it's all over we'll have the biggest damn party this world has ever seen."

"That we will, Rash'Tor'Ri."

I turned and walked toward the glow of the Great Gate. Kil'Sin'Deres stood beside the gate waiting.

"Time to start covering your mind glow, Rash'Tor'Ri," he said. "We are about to go back into danger. A group of humans with a group of Kresh is not uncommon. A single Human and a Farrara'Ti is less common. Calm your mind as we proceed."

"Alright," I said, "let's do it."

We stepped through the gate.

Chapter 18

"So, how do they get these big armies through the great gates so quickly?" I asked. "The streets were packed as we came in."

"The Gate facilities are on the outer ring of Hub. The back side of this building is open to the plains. When the gates are used for large numbers the back wall sinks into the ground and the Gate is available to all who are out on the plains."

"I get it," I said, "It actually makes sense. But then, what are all of the buildings inside of Hub used for?"

"There is a central building that supplies power to all the rest. The rest of them are used to house the clans of the ten Farrara'Ti who are in possession of the fourteen colonies."

"Shouldn't there be fourteen?"

"Several Farrara'Ti have two colonies."

"Ok," I said. "I've spent years afraid of the technology you guys had to have to be able to use portals, but you're just using the Makers' stuff, aren't you?"

"Sadly, yes," he said, "We are not the ones who created the technology. We use what is here and not much more. We do not know how to reset the Great Gates to different locations. They are set to the same settings they have been for thousands of years."

"Speakin of locations," I said, "can you tell me where the other locations are on Earth?"

"Sadly, I cannot." he said. "When I was the controller, I used small gates. I never used the Great Gates after the other facility was destroyed. I operated out of that one. I was lucky I was not there when the building was destroyed. Or perhaps, your ancestor was lucky I was not there."

"He was a tough bastard," I said.

"You have killed two Farrara'Ti by chance. It is much harder to kill Farrara'Ti than you may think."

We had been walking along the huge Avenue that circled around Hub and passed in front of every Gate facility. This route was less traveled that the other way we had come in.

"I can see where it might be a pretty tough task," I said.

"True," he said. "We have covered almost half of the distance, Rash'Tor'Ri. You will be home soon."

"I'm ready to be home," I said. "Lyrica is probably fuming because she didn't get to come."

"Frankly," I said, "if I'd known things were goin' to go so well, I wouldn't have put up a fight about it."

I knew right after I said it, it was a mistake. You just don't say stuff like that in the middle of a city on another world populated by a race that has dreams of killing you every night.

And I was right.

We walked around a corner and came face to face with a Farrara'Ti. He looked at me with his eyes narrowed. I could feel the mental probe and let out a long sigh.

"You are of the Blood. You carry no Mark. I always wanted a pet Bloodborn."

It was sudden. He began to Lash out with his Mark.

I ripped his Soul out of his body with my mind. For a fraction of a second, I was touching that Source. But I was out as quickly. I still felt that darkness grow with each time though.

Kil'Sin'Deres looked down at me with the most Human expression I had ever seen on a Kresh. His arms were spread with the palms up and the expression on his face was plain. What the Hell?

"What?" I asked.

He sighed.

There was a massive roar somewhere in Hub ahead of us.

"That didn't sound good," I said.

"No," he said, "it did not. I stand corrected, Rash'Tor'Ri. Apparently killing Farrara'Ti is easier than I thought. Much better if you had let me Mark him."

"Ah, shit," I said, "I wasn't thinkin' clearly. He was about to Mark me."

"Hmmm."

I could hear them coming and my monster wanted out of its cage.

"It has been ages since I have been in a battle," Kil'Sin'Deres said as he turned to face a horde of Kresh, pouring down the street.

"Me too," I said and let my beast out.

As they closed, my eyes glowed with the red fires of rage and I formed a Soulblade in each hand.

With an inhuman roar of rage I was into their midst. Beside me was Kil'Sin'Deres, and I learned why he would say that a Farrara'Ti would be considered hard to kill.

Once again, I found myself doing what I love. It's a sad thing that what I love is slaughtering my enemies. I'm certain that says something bad about me.

I charged forward, my blades cutting through flesh as if it were nothing. These were the lowest form of Kresh and we waded through them as if they weren't there. I saw soldiers and Wraiths at the rear, so I opened portals on my weapons and opened fire. Disks ripped across the street and tore through two Wraiths.

My Soullance fired straight down the street to blast a hole in the chest of a third. I kept firing it and passed it back and forth along the street.

"We must get you back home, Rash'Tor'Ri," Kil'Sin'Deres said. "We do not have time for this."

I beat my rage back down and looked up.

"Can you jump that far? From building to building?"

"Yes, can you?"

"Oh yeah," I said, "then it looks like I get to look at one of these buildings, after all. Let's get inside as soon as we get a break in these guys. They don't need to see us go in."

"Back around the corner then," Kil'Sin'Deres said. "We can go in the back door."

While the Kresh were distracted by the fire burning amongst them, we slipped back around the corner. He shot toward the other corner faster than anything I'd ever seen. I guess a Soulstream that is almost the size of Paige's does lend speed to someone. I followed, much faster than the Kresh that were coming toward the corner we had slipped behind. We hit the corner and didn't slow down.

About a third of the way down this side, he entered a door. I followed to find myself in a hallway that was decent sized for me but Kil'Sin'Deres had to hunch over quite a bit.

He was chuckling.

"What?"

"I was just thinking of the words you were saying right before we met Lod'Mar'Kovelag."

"Yeah," I said, "I coulda gone all day without sayin' something like that."

He chuckled again.

"The stairs are this way," he moved forward, stooped over.

"I see why you guys don't use these passages," I said.

"Very uncomfortable," he said, "The stairs are a little better, but not much."

We followed the hall for some time. I estimated it was about half way through the immense building. We exited into a central shaft with a stairway that wound around all four walls. I looked up.

"That's a long way up."

"The stairway will be cramped, but if I lean forward..."

"I got a better idea," I said.

I stepped out into the open area and jumped up a couple of floors and grabbed the railing. Then I threw myself up another floor or two.

"I like this idea," Kil'Sin'Deres said as he passed me, jumping up three or four floors at a time.

"So how do you know where everything's at up in here, when your people don't use it?"

"I was born Kresh'Sor'An," he said as I caught up with him. "I had nothing in common with those I was placed with. I spent much time exploring the places a Kresh child would fit. As I grew, I stopped my explorations."

The more I learned about Kil'Sin'Deres, the more I came to realize that he was far closer to Human than most of his race.

"I see," I said, "and how many floors are in one of these?"

"Three hundred and twelve in most of them," he said.

"How many Humans do you think could fit in a floor?"

"Three hundred or so," he said. "If you mean packed in close quarters, perhaps five hundred."

A person might hide fifteen thousand people inside one of these buildings if they were so inclined. There were a lot of buildings in Hub.

We continued upwards until there was an end to the stairs. I followed Kil'Sin'Deres out a door at the very top.

The lighting was still off kilter for me on Kresh. But that was one of the most memorable things I would ever see. I was looking across an endless sea of rooftops.

"We can stay on the outer ring," I said, "or we can make a straight line run for it."

"We should stay on the outer rim," he said. "There will be less chance of an adventurous Kresh wandering the upper levels."

"Around the edge it is," I said.

Chapter 19

I jumped across the span between the third and fourth building from where we had begun.

"We shoulda done this from the start," I said.

"It had not occurred to me, Rash'Tor'Ri," Kil'Sin'Deres said with a shrug, "and if we had, you would not have had the pleasure of killing a Farrara'Ti that had declared your race to be destroyed."

"He was a bad guy, then?" I asked.

"He was one of the two Farrara'Ti that vied for control of the facility to Earth. They were in contest over who would be the next clan to come to your world."

"I guess I made that decision for 'em," I said, "Dammit."

"Unfortunate," he said

"They could've argued for months yet."

"The other one, Jas'Por'Kadin is sneaky," he said. "There will be tricks, sneak attacks, or assassination attempts. He won't just pour his forces through the Gate to kill any they can. Lod'Mar'Kovelag was smarter. But either of them would scout and find the military forces that he could and set up surprise attacks."

"I don't like the sound of that."

"Of course, he was not smart enough *not* to try to Mark Rash'Tor'Ri," he said. "Perhaps you have earned the name."

"I guess so," I said, "I have a dilemma. How is it that you were the calm one during that fight back there? Your DNA is all Kresh. Mine is just a fraction and I have to beat down that monster inside me every time."

He laughed.

"I am two thousand years old," He said, "When you have lived that long with the war inside you, you will have learned a little restraint as well. You are still young."

"I can't even imagine what that's like," I said.

"How is it, Rash'Tor'Ri, that you can rip the life out of one of the most powerful of our race with nothing but your mind? It is something I have never encountered before and it is truly astonishing."

"That's part of my heritage from the other bloodline," I said. "Merlin could do it, too. The DNA you left me lets me cross the boundaries that would not have been possible before."

"As I said, astonishing."

"There is a downside," I said, "When I do that to one of your race, I come in contact with your Source. It adds changes to the DNA I carry quicker than just natural aging. It makes it harder to wrestle with my rage."

"I see," he said, "so every advantage has its price."

"True enough."

We continued our trek across the rooftops. I really didn't like the sound of this Jas'Por'Kadin, he sounded like the one who had brought in the

Shak'Tar. I really dislike that sort of thing. I'm pretty straight forward, when you think about it.

"There is our destination," Kil'Sin'Deres said as we stopped. He was pointing at the next building that looked pretty much like all the others.

"I'm glad you're here to show me," I said, "all these damn buildings look the same."

I opened my Sight and looked down at the flows of power inside the building. There were a lot of Kresh. A lot more than there had been when we came in. I couldn't see the Soul of another Farrara'Ti, though.

"There are thousands of Kresh piled in that building," I said. "I think our secret got out. They must know where we are heading."

"Not necessarily," he said. "They could be trying to overcome Lod'Mar'Kovelag's clan. They may be setting up to defend their right to hold it. It could be a number of things."

"Either way, we have a problem," I said. "We need a distraction and I have an idea."

"I spent some time talking to your Sam Keller," he said. "He warned me that things might get complicated if I ever heard those particular words from you."

"We have a problem?"

"No, 'I have an idea' was the phrase he told me to watch out for."

"I can't believe he'd say something like that," I said, "It hurts my feelin'."

The expression I got from him I had seen many times on the faces of my friends and family. He just looked at me with one eyebrow, or sort of a scaly ridge in his case, raised.

I couldn't stop myself from letting out a short giggle. It's all I could call it. It couldn't be called anything else, and I was really happy that Prada hadn't been there to see it, or Jacobs. I'd never hear the end of it.

"I have learned much about you over the last few days, Rash'Tor'Ri," he said with a grin. "Perhaps Humans are just too delicate for your antics. I look forward to hearing this wonderful idea you have devised."

"Where might we find this Jas'Por'Kadin?" I asked.

"He would be in the fourth building in toward the center of Hub, I would guess. That building has been the place where the Farrara'Ti has stayed for the facility for Earth. He should be inside that building or somewhere between here and there."

"What say we go find his sneaky ass and give him a little of his own?"

"I like this idea," he said, "so follow me."

We headed across the building toward the center of Hub. We jumped over three avenues and stopped. We stood atop the building and I looked down inside with my Sight. Sure enough, I could see one of the Souls that rolled with power like Kil'Sin'Deres' Soul.

"You can throw power like a Ma'Nar, can't you?" I asked.

"A Ma'Nar wishes he could throw power," he said.

"Alright, this is what I wanna do," I said, "I'm gonna do something loud and when he comes outside, we blast him with everything we both have. Then we haul ass back to the Gate and head down when they thin out."

"Sounds fun," he said, "but they will head up the building after us quickly."

"Then we'll head in toward the center of the city so they think that's our direction."

"Do it."

I looked across at the building opposite us. I began building an intricate shield. When it was done I pushed it out with my mind to settle inside the solid side of the building, about halfway up the side.

"Ready?"

"Yes."

I Pulled hard from the Source and poured it into that shield. I wasn't sure how much it would take to do the job. Apparently, the more solid the object, the quicker the reaction.

When a Soulguard imbues his weapon with Soulfire, it is a coating of the Soul over the weapon. When Soulfire is forced inside of a solid, well, it's a bit explosive. Lyrica and I had dropped a mountain on the Gate in Romania this way.

The side of the building went white hot and the explosion knocked us both backwards and the building shook below us.

"Rash'Tor'Ri," Kil'Sin'Deres said with his eyes wide.

"That was a little bigger than I expected."

We jumped up and returned to the edge. I saw the Soul of our target exit the building.

"Now."

I Pulled again from the Source and cut loose with every weapon I had. Disks and lance slammed downward and then there was a stream of purple and black fireballs right alongside them. The sheer amount of power he used was breathtaking, and I could feel his Pull just as strongly as I could have felt a Pull from Paige.

If Jas'Por'Kadin had not been distracted by the huge letters blown into the walls of the building across the street, he may have been able to move in time. But every eye in the street was on the huge letters. Both of our attacks hit him undefended, and he was blown to ashes in seconds.

We stopped and leaped across the avenue to the building I had used as the distraction. We made sure they saw us.

There was a second mass roar that thundered across Hub.

I may have let another giggle slip. Thank God Jacobs and Prada were on Earth.

We began running toward the center of Hub. Each time we jumped an avenue, we slowed to make sure they knew what direction we were moving.

"Left."

I said and we switched directions. We sped up to nearly seventy miles per hour, and jumped fast as we could to spend as little time as we could between buildings. Then we stopped about four buildings away from our destination and entered the building.

The trip down was much quicker than the one we had made up to the first roof top. Then we exited by the back door of this one.

We walked the distance remaining along the street with other Kresh as hordes poured out of the area toward the center of Hub. Their eyes toward the sky.

"Hope the next guy is dumb as a rock," I said.

Kil'Sin'Deres chuckled.

As we approached the building we wanted, the hordes seemed to have finally finished running out of the doors.

We walked in as if we were supposed to be there and headed toward a side passage that led toward one of the rooms with a small gate.

Someone must have seen us because I could see the horde's Souls reverse course and head back toward the facility.

"Oh shit," I said, "they're on their way back."

"Does not matter," Kil'Sin'Deres said. "We are here."

"Rash'Tor'Ri," a voice came from the darkness and I felt one of the Shak'Tar, "I have come with a report but it seems the passages are blocked out of the facility."

"You come with me through the gate," I said. "Let's go Kil'Sin'Deres."

"I think I will stay and take care of this mess. There are two clans of unmarked Kresh running around here."

"You'll have to fight your way to one of the Ma'Nar before you Mark. Just come with us."

I saw the smile on his face as he turned to the roaring mass coming down the halls. I stepped up beside him as the gate opened behind me.

"I'm not leavin' you to fight all those bastards alone."

The beast was clawing at my mental walls and Soulfire began to roll across my body.

"Go home, and prepare yourselves."

Kil'Sin'Deres literally picked me up and threw me through the gate with a roar of laughter.

I hit the ground rolling with Soulfire pouring across my body and two Soulblades in my hands. I came to my feet with a snarl, and started back toward the gate to find the Shak'Tar pushed through and the gate closed.

I stood staring at the empty space for a minute, then beat the rage down and let the flames die around me.

I turned around to find five people standing in front of a wrecked picnic lunch. Lyrica, Paige, Kyra, and Mattie all stood with their hands on their hips with that, oh so familiar, look. Prada was just shaking her head.

"What?"

"Secret mission," Paige said. "What part of that didn't you understand?"

"It's not my fault," I said.

"Sure it's not,"

"Seriously, it was just bad luck."

"Sure."

Paige shook her head, "Welcome home."

Lyrica was in my arms as soon as she was sure Paige was through berating me.

She was staring into my eyes as she watched all that had occurred in Hub. I extended my telepathy out so all of them could see what happened. It was similar to one of the Shak'Tar's memory dumps. I figured it would save time.

"You wrote it on the walls of a building in the middle of the biggest city on their world?" Kyra asked.

"It seemed appropriate," I said.

"True enough," Mattie said.

Chapter 20

The Prophet led Bel and her squad up through the stairway of the building. She couldn't believe what they had become capable of in the short time since she had learned how to tie her Soulstream into the knot.

"Why are we climbing the stairs of a building in the heart of the Master's city?" Seldin asked.

"Do not question orders, Seldin," Bel said.

"It's ok, Bel," the Prophet said. "I've heard rumors of something very interesting that occurred yesterday. I want to see it for myself. I felt you would enjoy it as well, so here we are."

"What is it, Prophet?"

"We'll see, together, Bel," he said with a grin.

She followed as the Prophet jumped up through the center of the stairwell that led from the bottom to the top of the building. He cleared several stories and grabbed a railing. Then he launched upwards for another.

Bel and her squad of nine of The Prophet's Guard launched themselves upwards as the Prophet had done.

When they reached the top of the building, they exited onto the roof.

Bel had never been this high except when climbing cliffs. She looked out in awe at the sea of rooftops that she saw leading off into the distance.

"It should be on the East end of the building," the Prophet said and walked to the left.

He looked over the edge and his shoulders started to shake. Bel thought he was sobbing for a second.

"Prophet?" she asked in worry.

He turned with a wide grin on his face and she realized it was laughter instead of sobbing that shook his shoulders. He slowly just sat down with his back leaning against the escarpment and laughed.

She stepped up to the edge and looked down.

Her squad were some of the highest educated of her people. Since the Prophet had found them, they had learned to read and write. The Prophet said it was a useful skill and she took his words to heart.

What she saw brought a great smile to her face. In huge letters, created by holes blown in the side of the building was a single word.

Rash'Tor'Ri.

She heard the Prophet muttering under his breath in the language she was in the process of learning, the language of the Prophet.

"Crazy son of a bitch."

***

I sat behind a desk at the Academy in Montana. The gate had dropped me off at the same spot where we had set off nearly a week before.

There had been people stationed at all times in the clearing to be there when I returned.

Pure luck had played a part in who had been there to greet me.

They had just replaced the squad that had been standing guard only about fifteen minutes before I had been hurled through the gate.

"So let me have it," I said. "Who is this Prophet and what's he doin' with the people who disappear?"

I watched his report in his mind.

They had found the prophet within a day's travel of Hub. They snuck into his camp and bypassed his guards.

Both Ritte and Kol had been Shak'Tar I had met before. They were a couple of the original ones I had Marked in Romania.

Both men slipped into the Prophet's tent to find him standing across the tent. His back was to them, and he held a sword in each hand. He was working through several stances that were very familiar to me.

"Better be a good reason you snuck into my tent," the voice was very familiar to me as well.

It couldn't be.

"We come from Rash'Tor'Ri," Jag said. "We have come to find out what is going on with the disappearing humans."

"And why would you care?"

"Our Master doesn't wish humans to be hurt in his name. If you are working for the Kresh and causing hurt to the Humans of this world, we will remove you."

"Two brave souls," the Prophet said, "but there's no reason to have issue with me. I am hiding Humans from their former Masters and I am training an army to join Rash'Tor'Ri when he comes here."

"I feel the truth of your words Prophet. We were given orders with this outcome in mind as well."

"And what are those orders?" the Prophet asked and turned around to face the two men.

"No Friggin' way!" I interrupted the report.

"Master, what is it?"

"Whatever that man asks for, you give," I said. "Any help he needs, he gets. From Shak'Tar, Human, or Kresh. Any of my clans are to support the Prophet. The people he is hiding can be taken to Cerres. Make sure he knows everything that occurred there."

"You know him," Ritte said.

"Damn right, I know him and I thought he was dead," I said. "Just info dump the rest on me and get back there as soon as possible. Get word to the Prophet, Gorvelis, and Kil'Sin'Deres. This guy is to be protected."

"Yes Master," he said and dropped the information on me and turned around. He left quickly.

I sat back in thought and Lyrica walked in to find me sitting there with a goofy grin on my face.

I said two words to her, "He's alive!"

My friend lives.

Rictor Hughes had somehow been sucked into that gate he had blown up and come out over there and they call him Prophet.

Chapter 21

"We've hit a stumbling block with the weapons," Warren said.

"I'm guessin' that there's a lot of people who can't use 'em," I answered.

"How did you know?"

"The Makers over on Kresh use a tech like this," I said. "I found out that only about twenty five percent of the people they stuffed into the machines could make 'em work. I figured we would have even worse odds."

"In fact," he said, "we have a little better odds than that. About thirty percent of them were able to use it. It didn't slow the orders. The US is forming a cadre of Source gunners and incorporating it into their tactics."

"I'm glad they can still use 'em at all. I wanted to arm the whole world with the guns but I'll settle for what I can get."

"We've sent test parts to find which men can use the interface. They'll be ready to start training as the guns start rolling in."

"How soon can we get 'em shipped out?" I asked.

"Within the week, the first shipment starts going out from McMinnville."

"Good," I said, "and how about the one overseas?"

"It goes online tomorrow, Sir."

"Excellent," I said. "Maybe I set 'em back enough to get us some more time. We need to speed it up as much as we can."

"I've got three shifts working seven days a week in McMinnville. We received the first payments on the US contract, and I bought another plant close to the first. It should be ready to start production before month's end."

"You're a Godsend, Warren," I said. "Don't know what we'd do without ya."

"You'd probably bankrupt yourself buying food."

"You're probably right," I said with a laugh.

"What did you mean when you said you set them back?"

"They had two Farrara'Ti who couldn't decide which was gonna try to take a piece of us. So we killed 'em both."

"I see," he said.

"It wasn't my fault."

He looked at me with one eyebrow raised.

"Why's everybody keep lookin' at me like that?" I grumbled.

***

"More wings, please," I said to the waitress.

"It figures," she said. "Carol told me about you guys."

I was guessing that Carol was the waitress who had been there on our last visit to Hooters.

"How about the extra large gentlemen?" she asked, looking at Kharl and Dietrich Jaegher.

"Yep," Kharl said and Dietrich nodded to her.

"Thought so," she said. "How 'bout the rest of you?"

"I'll take another round," Trent said.

He and Mattie had adapted to their new Soulstreams quickly and were on the rolls as Mageguards. Both were working on their shield skills as much as possible.

"I brought you guys out to celebrate something I found out while I was over there," I said as the waitress headed back to the kitchen. "Well, several things, actually. One is a personal discovery, and the other is something that affects all of us."

"Spit it out," Kharl said.

"I learned there is a guy runnin' around over there they call the Prophet of Rash'Tor'Ri. He is going from village to village, and the people who live there follow him and disappear. We sent a couple of agents to find out what was going on. They found the Prophet and discovered that he is training an army over there in some hidden facility that the Kresh don't know anything about."

"He's not only training them, but showing them how to knot their Soulstreams."

"A Soulguard?" Dietrich asked.

"Not just any Soulguard either," I said, "We all know him. I'm goin' to show you a memory from the agent's report."

I used my telepathy that seems to get stronger each year. I showed them an image of the Prophet as he turned around to face the agents.

"Son of a bitch!" Prada said.

"I'll second that," Kharl said with a smile. "He looks a little worse for wear, but it's Ric."

"He apparently didn't go unscathed but he's alive and kickin'," I said.

"And of course, building an army in the center of hundreds of millions of Kresh," Kyra said. "He'll conquer the whole damn world if we don't hurry up and get done here."

I chuckled along with several of the others.

"I've instructed all of my people to help him, and help hide those he protects."

"Good call, Son," Kharl said.

"Your people," Kyra said, "means a lot more than it used to doesn't it?"

Mom is perceptive. She'd seen a difference in me almost as quickly as Lyrica had. I had never had a longing for anything but battle for most of my years.

"Yes it does," I said.

"There is another army building out there to join us as well. The 'people' I'm talkin' about are a planet full of Humans that are joining the ranks of the Soulguard as fast as they can be trained. Which is pretty quick considering that the first of the recruits are telepathic. They'll learn at an astonishing rate and they can teach just as fast."

"While that is building," I said, "Kil'Sin'Deres is building the clans up by spreading the Mark to the smaller clans. He's growing my clans to be able to face the others and take Kresh."

"You've been busy," Dietrich said. "Can you trust the Kresh?"

"That's one of the things I can say for certain. They live by the Mark. They carry my Mark and they won't betray me. They're loyal."

"Actually," I said, "there's an easy way to show you. I'm goin' to give you one of the info dumps like the Shak'Tar do. It's not harmful. You can literally relive what happened over there though."

I used the telepathy again, and let them see all that happened from the time I left to the time I returned to the glade in Montana.

"That's an interesting skill," Dietrich said, "and useful."

"I agree," I said, "although it's a little disconcerting when you're surrounded by telepathic people who do it all the time. Silent conversations and stuff. Sam has been bitchin', nonstop since he got to Cerres. 'Use your words, Dammit!' would echo across the square pretty regular."

"I could see that," Trent said with a grin.

"He's gonna have so much fun over there," Kharl laughed.

"You had to kick the hornet's nest, I see," Mattie said as she was watching the return trip home.

"It wasn't my fault."

She looked at me with one eyebrow raised.

"Why's everybody keep lookin' at me like that?"

"I wonder," Trent said. "I have to say, the graffiti was a nice touch."

"I thought so."

"I guess if the plan is to keep 'em lookin' in our direction," Kharl said, "that'll do it."

"Any word on how that's playin' out?" Dietrich asked.

"Not yet," I said. "Kil'Sin'Deres said he was about to go Mark both of their clans and pull out of the area. I'm hopin' we get lucky with the next one to step in."

"Never thought I'd say this, but that Kil'Sin'Deres is a likable sort," Dietrich said.

"Yeah, it was so much easier to hate 'em all when they were a faceless horde of monsters," I said.

"I'm proud of what you've done, Son," Kyra said. "You've hated them with ample reason your whole life and you put it aside long enough to do something like this."

"Thanks, Mom," I said.

Lyrica squeezed my hand. She is the reason I can do what Kyra is talking about. When I'm with Lyrica, I don't want to be a monster, and it influences every decision I have made since I joined my life with hers.

It really is easier to hate them all.

Chapter 22

It had been three months since I had gotten back from my trip through the rabbit hole, and I still hadn't heard from the other side of the gate. I was beginning to worry. What if they had been caught? What if the Kresh were slaughtering my people on Cerres?

I shook my head and tried to clear my thoughts. I was out by the gate in the middle of the Dance of Blades. Otep was screaming in my ears, and my rage was pouring out through my walls. I can bleed off a lot of rage while I practice, but sometimes I get a little carried away.

Arcs of power slammed outward from my swords as they blurred with speed. Power hammered the earth all around the spot where the gate had opened twice before. If I could have opened it from this side, I would have just to get at them.

I finally stopped and just stood there, staring into that spot. I looked down into the Source as I usually did while out here. I looked for some reason why it was this spot.

Kil'Sin'Deres had said they didn't know how to set the Great Gates to a different location. I wondered if that was because there was something unique about the spot. But I still could find no discernable difference from any other spot I have looked at.

Except, now, this spot was on fire.

I felt Pelin approaching. I could feel the caution she was taking. The Shak'Tar understand my rage more than anyone. They share a piece of it themselves. We all have the Kresh DNA in our blood. What they don't have is the ability to touch that Source and kick that DNA in the ass. It has already changed me more than a normal Bloodborn changes in a lifetime.

"It's fine Pelin," I said. "My tantrum is done."

"We worry about you, Master," she said. "The Blood affects you more than it does most of us."

"I worry 'bout it too, Pelin," I said, "I just have to do the best I can until..."

"Until what?"

"Nevermind," I said, "it's just a pipe dream. What's goin' on?"

"We have a report from Hub," she said. "You have been worried of late and I thought you would like to know immediately."

"Kil'Sin'Deres Marked both clans from which you removed their Farrara'Ti. He has moved them into the Cerres Facility and the surrounding buildings."

"Good," I said. "I'm glad he got out of the Earth Facility, or Doran, whichever you would rather call it."

"He also moved his clans into Hub and took a second facility," she said. "He took Fuegass and the small clan that was holding it. Now he must remain quiet for a short time so as not to draw more attention to them."

"I can see that," I said. "So we control the access to two other worlds, one of which, is controlled by my people."

"They have sent emissaries from Cerres to Fuegass. They will not Mark any Humans but they will begin to unify the population of that colony. Be warned, some may request to be Marked after they find out the whole truth about what is happening. I know you don't want this but it is something we will have to deal with."

"I understand," I said, "but I don't want anyone Marked until they have been given the knowledge to make that choice. I want them to see what freedom is before they just jump in with a new Master."

"It will be done, Master."

"Don't call me Master."

"Yes, Master," she said with a grin.

I just let out a long sigh that just caused a larger grin from Pelin.

"Anything from the Prophet?" I asked.

"The first groups of refugees he has pulled from the villages on Kresh have begun to arrive in Hub. They are beginning to funnel them into Cerres to keep them safe. After a time Fuegass will be available to them as well."

"It seems your friend is wasting no time," she said. "He has a group of nearly five hundred men and women who have knotted their streams as your Soulguard. They work with the Prophet to protect their charges."

"The man is dedicated," I said. "He sees people in need and he will help."

"Some of his people have come to Cerres and begun training with your group there. Once he found out they were there, he be began sending them to Keller for their training. It freed him up to find more people and get them out of harm's way."

"How many Humans are on Kresh, I wonder."

"Millions," she said, "possibly billions. Kresh is about the size of your world. But where yours is three quarters water, Kresh is three quarters land. There is a lot of space to fill."

"Wow, it looks like Ric has a big job ahead of him."

"Very big," she said.

"I almost hate to ask, but has another Kresh taken up residence at the Doran facility?"

"Yes," she said. "His name is Gal'Vor'Hadon and he is powerful. He has a large clan and he will use them. He has fewer of the Ma'Nar, but more of the lower classes than some of them. But his clans are closer to ideal to face what we have on Earth. He'll flood the world with sheer numbers."

"If they're the lower classes, our troops have a better chance of facing 'em," I said. "I guess I need to spread the word about what to expect. Any guesses about when he'll come through?"

"Kil'Sin'Deres says to expect attacks to begin within the next three months. It doesn't give us much time to ready our forces."

"Better than the last time we had prior warning," I said. "Several days warning was all we got. We knew where it would be though. This time we have to wait."

"This will be the last agent through the gate for a while. Are there any special messages you wish to send?" she asked.

"Just what we've talked about," I said. "Tell them I am proud they are my clan and that I could ask for no better."

"It will be done."

As Pelin walked away, I thought of the short time we had left before the world would be under attack. So much to do and a small time to do it in. I would call Warren. We needed to speed up production of the Source Weapons.

I looked at the spot where the Gate had been, as the fires I had started died off, and started back toward the base. I had to meet with Paige and Gregor, Marco and Polo, and tell Lyrica what was happening.

Chapter 23

"Three months," Paige said, "That just sucks."

"That it does," I said.

"With no clue where the gate will open?" Gregor asked.

"None," I said, "but we know it won't be Romania. We doubt it will be here but we have to be prepared in case it is here. Frankly, there's not much we can do to prepare."

"We'll warn everyone," Paige said. "We can tell them that the Kresh will be in high numbers, and that the lower forms are vulnerable to gunfire."

"It's the best we can do," Gregor said. "Keep our forces on alert and be prepared to join the battle as soon as we find out where to go."

"Now I'm headin' over to see Marco and Polo," I said. "I'll let 'em know what's goin' on."

"Good," Paige said, "and we'll start making calls to put the word out. I just wish we had more time."

"It wouldn't have mattered when they came," I said. "We would always wish for more time. Although, I wish we had more of the Source Weapons out there."

"Very true," Gregor said.

"Good luck with the politics," I said as I stood and left the room.

As I made my way toward Marco and Polo's offices, I heard a song. Someone was playing Lime in the Coconut loudly outside the new barracks for our support Mages.

I saw the guy laying on a lounge chair designed from a shield outside the barracks with a drink in his hand.

What caught my eye, more than anything else, was the spot the music was coming from. To the naked eye, it was coming from nowhere, but my Sight picked out the source of the music at once. The man had created speakers from a set of intricate shields.

Just the focus necessary for something like that was ridiculous. I don't think I could do it with the ability to see what I was doing, much less with the limitations of a Mage.

I cleared my throat and the Mage opened his eyes. He was on his feet, immediately.

"Yes, Sir," he said quickly.

The music stopped.

"What's your name?" I asked.

"Jack, Sir."

"Jack, that's the damnedest focus skills I've ever seen. How did you do that with shields?"

"Um, I'm kinda good with engineering, Sir."

"It's just Colin, Jack," I said. "If you can do that kind of detail with a speaker, I have a job for ya."

"Whatever you need, Sir... Colin."

"Come with me," I said. "I want you with Jacobs. What kind of engineering are you good with?"

"Almost any kind," he said as he started regaining his composure, "'cause I'm older than I look. I have degrees from twelve different colleges over the last sixty years."

"Holy shit, and where have you been all this time?" I asked. "You shoulda been busy for the last few years."

"I've been in Japan for the last two years," he said. "I just got back to the States a month ago."

"I can guarantee you'll be busy from here on out," I said. "Jacobs will appreciate a guy like you.

"Uh... thanks."

After I left him with a thoroughly pleased Jacobs, I headed back toward the offices I was previously aimed for. I might have uses for Jack the Engineer myself. I would definitely get him in touch with Warren and see what he could do with enough money to back him. The outcome could be quite interesting.

Marco and Polo were waiting in front of the building in which they held offices.

"Colin," Marco said, "I understand we have a time frame to work with?"

"Vaguely," I said, "within three months is what Kil'Sin'Deres estimated. We know the guy is strong and has a lot of Kresh in his clans. It's gonna be ugly. He'll pour millions of his Kresh on us and try to take us with numbers. One advantage we have is that most of his Kresh are of the lower classes. Bullets will work with the majority of the Kresh."

"Still limited effect with the Soldiers, though," Polo said, "and it sounds like those will be plentiful as well."

"True," I said, "There's really not goin' to be an easy way to stop 'em, guys. It's gonna get bloody."

"If they come out here we'll destroy 'em," Marco said. "It's a pretty safe bet they won't come out here."

"I don't expect 'em here, but I have to stay here so the lure is still here. It might be the only way we could coax 'em out close," I said. "I need to move to Edinburgh so I can respond quicker, but it would move the lure to a spot where we aren't ready."

"We'll get with the President and see if we can start consolidating our forces in Europe at Edinburgh. We'll get them on high alert and ready. It's probably the best we can do. This Soulgunner Corps is growing, and they're being incorporated in all the units we have."

"It's a shame that only about a third of our troops have been able to use the Soulgun," Polo said. "It'll limit us but a third is better than none. We still have about twenty five thousand Soulgunners in the American forces. Nearly ten thousand of those are National Guard. I think we'll be sending at least half of those to Edinburgh, as well."

"Those numbers seem to be carrying on through the other countries as well," I said, "except, oddly, China. They have a nearly seventy percent success rate."

"Is there anything that can explain why?" asked Polo.

"Not that we can find," I said. "It just seems to work that way. Since the attacks, their army is probably the largest in the entire world. Maybe not the best trained, but the best armed for this war."

"Warren has five plants working twenty four hours a day, seven days a week. He's signed some contracts to sub out the barrels to the Springfield Arms Company, too. They're taking over the replacement barrel operation. We receive finished barrels in a totally separate plant and our Soulguards are installin' the shield lenses."

"That's impressive, considering it's only been a few months since you began," Marco said.

"It's time sensitive and we're runnin' out of it. Especially now. Warren has spent a shitload of money expanding the operation. I told him to keep it goin'. I don't need the money, I just blow shit up."

"That's what I hear," Polo said, "and I understand you blew a few things up on your secret mission a few months ago. Someone told me you left a rather large piece of graffiti on the walls of Hub."

"It seemed appropriate."

"The operating term was 'secret mission'," he said, "and thus it implies a mission that nobody knows happened."

"They don't know anything about the mission," I said. "They just know I can reach them when I so choose, and remove them from this mortal coil."

"And where'd you get that particular phrase?"

"I've been dying to use that in a sentence," I said.

"I'd say so," Marco said, "and it's a pretty good phrase."

"I think so," I said. "It ranks up there with 'Woe is me'. How often do ya get to hear that one used?"

"By the way," Polo said, "am I to understand that you signed a contract with certain Middle Eastern governments that we are on the verge of open war with for your weapons? This comes from the White House and they are not pleased."

"They signed contracts," I said. "The Source Weapons will not be used on other Humans."

"You know they can't be trusted," he said, "They'll follow the contract only as long as it suits them."

"Don't worry," I said, "the contract will be enforced. They try to use the weapons on Humans, they'll lose the gun."

"I just don't see how you'll be able to enforce it."

"It's enforced already, Seran," I said, "just trust me."

"I'm trying," he said, "but all I see is stronger weapons in the hands of people who have sworn to destroy this country."

"We have bigger fish to fry, now," I said, "so have a little faith in Humanity and let's just get ready for an Alien Apocalypse."

I turned and headed toward home, "Now I gotta tell my lady about the impending Apocalypse, I'll see ya later. All I can say is just trust me."

I could see the doubt in both men's auras, but they would understand soon enough. The Human race had to unite as a Race or we would die.

As I approached, I could sense a disturbed Soul awaiting me.

"Can you explain this to me?" Lyrica asked as I walked into our quarters on base.

She handed me an envelope. I opened it to find a check for a rather large amount.

"I guess I forgot to tell ya about that," I said.

"About the fact that I would receive a check for some ungodly amount of money. You knew about it?"

"Frankly, I'm surprised you hadn't picked that particular memory to watch over the last few months. I guess I should tell you when you become a third owner in a company that is selling arms around the world."

"But, why?" she asked. "I'm not doing anything for the company."

"You've been working for no pay for the Soulguard for close to fifteen years, Honey," I said. "Without the things you learned in that time and taught me, that company may well have never existed.

"You work every day in the hospital in Wichita and never ask for a cent. They won't offer to pay you until you ask them to and you won't. So now you'll be paid for the things you would never ask to be paid for. You never have to ask to be paid for anything you decide to do for the Soulguard or the Hospital.

"What this job requires of you is to be the same beautiful human being you've always been, both inside and out."

She was in my arms and I felt the wetness on my shirt as she cried.

"I love you," was the only thing I heard.

"And I love you, my Little Angel."

"I don't need that much money."

"Too bad," I said, "That's the check you have for the last quarter. The next one will be similar."

"That's for a quarter?"

"Yep."

"Holy... Wow!"

"Enjoy it, Love. We may be overrun with Kresh in a few months. The whole idea of wealth could be lost after what's comin'."

Chapter 24

"You are so much like Merlin, it is frightening," Dietrich said. "He would plan and plot, forever trying to guess what would happen next."

"I want to be ready to do the maximum damage to the ones who are brave enough to poke their heads out here," I said. "I don't expect 'em to come here but, if they do, they're toast."

"I don't doubt that for a second, Colin."

We stood overlooking the battlefield we had left as a molten wasteland not so long ago. Grass had grown back already and it looked deceptively peaceful. It could all change in an instant and we were as prepared as we could be for that very outcome.

"Did you happen to see where Merlin crossed over into Hub while you were there?"

"Unfortunately, no," I said. "I was told where the empty spot was but it was over twenty miles in the other direction. I wanted to go but there wasn't time. Perhaps we can go look at it after we win this."

"Do you truly expect to win this?"

"We have to," I said. "Too many people are depending on it. Not just this world, but fourteen others. Two of those worlds are under the control of my forces already."

"He never dreamed there was so much beyond the Demon onslaught," Dietrich said. "Perhaps if he'd known, he would have chosen a different path."

"Perhaps," I said, "but the path he took appeals to me more than it's comfortable to think about. I could walk through that gate and end this war on Earth before it really begins. Do I have the right to do so? I don't think so."

"Was he weak to choose as he did?"

"Far from it," I said. "He thought he was dying for his world to be free. He thought he was ending the Demons' ability to come here. Given the knowledge he had at the time, I think it was one of the most selfless acts a man could make."

"I've thought of the same thing. If I didn't know of the other worlds out there of Humans, if I wasn't personally responsible for nearly sixty million beings on the other side of the gate, I would like to think I am strong enough to do the same."

"I know he was devastated by the loss of so many when Kent was slain, but you may be giving more credit than he deserves. He could have done what you are doing, and prepared more for the fight."

"I read the journal," I said. "He truly thought he could save this world with the sacrifice of himself alone. He tried, and if things had been as they are on several of the colonies, he would've succeeded. There were spots in the journal where, if you read between the lines, he was protecting more than just Earth. There are hints of the 'others' depending on him. His family."

"I lost much faith in our cause when he chose to walk away," Dietrich said, "but I am regaining my faith as I watch what you have done."

"I know what it's like to lose faith in someone," I said. "For years I never understood my father's actions. I blamed him for running off and dying in some grand display of revenge. I learned, later, the reason he'd done it. He did it so they'd think I was dead. He did that for me, so I could grow up and learn how to protect myself. Now it's my duty to make his sacrifice worthy. I'll see the Human race free or I'll die trying."

"That is why my faith in our cause is returning," Dietrich said, "and perhaps my faith in my friend, Merlin, is returning as well. I thank you for that."

Dietrich stood and walked away.

I hadn't really been aware how the big man felt about Merlin. I would have shared whatever insight I had gained from the journal long before.

I stood up as well, as it was almost time to meet at Cristof Damaris' residence. He was making dinner for us, a Greek dish called Moussaka. He claimed it was delicious and we were about to put that to the test.

My ten Mage Captains would be there as well as Lyrica and myself. I just hoped he made plenty, I was starving.

I reached Cristof's home on base a few minutes after Adaya and Alexei. The rest hadn't made it yet. Lyrica was supposed to be here in a few moments. She'd finished at the hospital and had already been home to clean up.

"Adaya, Alexei, how goes it?"

"It would be better if I had my Vodka," Alexei said, "But Cris claims that this silly fruit drink is what one must drink with his Greek food."

"You mean wine?"

"Yes, a silly fruit drink."

I laughed.

"Savage," Adaya said. "When you try to instill culture in the barbarians, this is what you have. No appreciation for a five hundred dollar bottle of wine."

I took a sip from the glass that Cristof placed in my hand.

"I'm afraid I have to agree with Alexei on this one," I said.

"Bloody Americans," came the voice of our resident Brit, Galen Stone. "Simply no understanding of a civilized meal."

"I am Russian and proud to stand with my American brother on this!" Alexei boomed.

"Alexei, I have a little something I picked up in Tennessee, last month," I said and I pulled quart jar from the box I had carried in with me.

"I think you might appreciate it more than these civilized pansies."

"I have heard of this," Alexei said with a smile, "and they say it is very hardy."

"Moonshine is pretty stout," I said. "Give it a shot."

"That it is."

"Good God," came Prada's voice from the door. "Don't drink that, Alexei. It's just one step from gasoline. Why would you do that to him, Colin?"

"Another of the pansies," I said. "Drink up."

Alexei took a swallow from the jar. After he took a deep breath he smiled.

"This is what I am talking about," he said. He made a shooing gesture at Prada. "Go drink the fruity pansy drink."

"No beer?"

"Madre de Dios!" Reyna said as she walked in. "Beer? You never drink beer with Moussaka. It must be a red wine."

"I'd rather have tea, if you don't mind," Lyrica said from behind her.

"Time to kick back and sink some tinnies," Brighton said as he walked in with a twelve pack of beer.

"I have no idea what you just said but I think we should relax and drink some beers," Trent said as he also walked in.

Brighton sighed and reached into the box. He pulled a Bud from it and pitched it to Trent. Another went to Prada. Mattie shook her head and pointed at Lyrica.

"I'm with her," she said. "I think I'd like some tea."

"I'll make you a cup," Stone said, "with cream and sugar?"

"Cris, don't you have some in the fridge?" asked Lyrica.

"Bloody American Savages. Cold tea?"

"With ice," Mattie said.

"A travesty, I say," Stone said, shaking his head.

It had been a while since I could take a moment and just enjoy watching the interaction of this bunch. They reminded me of the guys in Tennessee, back at my first post. Soldiers are soldiers, wherever they come from. The ones I seem to end up with are just more full of shit than most, I guess. Or maybe not, maybe all soldiers are full of shit.

The Moussaka was delicious and the company was awesome. What more could you ask for?

World peace? But then, what would we do for a living? We'd be out of a job.

Chapter 25

The ringing phone woke me up.

"Hello."

"It happened," Warren said. "One of the Reps has demanded reimbursement."

"The failsafe?"

"I would have to say more than likely," he said. "Two thousand guns malfunction at the same time."

"Get all the Reps together," I said, "and I'll be there this evening. I'm bringin' Marco and Polo as well. Might as well ease their concerns on the matter."

"We'll be expecting you."

"Ok, see ya then."

I hung up the phone. I knew it would happen. I'd hoped it wouldn't, but who was I kidding. We've been fighting amongst ourselves for thousands of years. Did I really expect it to change?

It had to change, or we were going to die.

"What is it?" Lyrica asked.

"Some idiot triggered the failsafe on the guns. I have to go to Tennessee. Are ya covered up at the hospital?"

"Unfortunately I am."

"I'll try not to blow anything up."

"Good luck with that," she said as I rolled out of our bed and headed for the bathroom.

After I talked with Marco and Polo, I was sure I could get by with using one of the planes for the trip to Nashville, since they would want to be there.

As it turned out, Paige and Gregor came, too, so I got to use the Soulguard jet.

***

"It has come to my attention, ladies and gentlemen," I said as I looked at the group of people from various nations around the world, "that one of you has an issue with my weapons."

"Very true," was the answer from the representative who had made the complaint.

His nation had been at war with its neighbor for as long as I could remember and I had figured there was a strong possibility of this very problem.

"You claim that two thousand Source weapons malfunctioned, simultaneously."

"That is true," he said. "We demand reimbursement for your faulty product!"

"And yet you'll get nothing," I said with my rage leaking through, "because you signed the contract that these weapons would not be used on other Humans. You defaulted on that contract when you tried to use them in that very manor."

"Lies! You have no proof of this!"

Do you honestly think you can lie to a telepath? I asked inside the heads of every person in the room. All eyes were riveted on me.

They had taken my guns and went straight to their neighboring country and tried to attack. I could see the memory of the reports. The reports of failed weapons. Of guns melting from the heat that erupted from the inside of the stock.

"Not only can you not lie to me," I said, "but I can show everyone here the memories of said lies."

"This is what you will receive," I said. "I will send you the same amount of weapons you bought before after you have paid the price quoted for those weapons again. You will sign the same contract as you signed before. If you try to use the weapons on Humans again, they will also fail."

"Ridiculous!"

"Then you will receive nothing," I said. "Read your contracts. All of you. If the attempt to use these weapons on Humans is made, you will lose said weapons. Did you think I wouldn't enforce the contracts? These weapons are for the protection of our world from the Kresh."

"Furthermore," I said, "if a second attempt is made, you will not only lose the weapon, but there will be no support from the Soulguard in the future. You are on your own."

I had discussed this portion of the meeting with Paige and Gregor. Gregor had been the one to actually suggest it. Paige agreed, but the whole subject was worrisome. The Soulguard protects Humanity. It would be a hard choice if we truly had to make it.

I could see shock on some faces. Some still held their facial expressions in check. But I could see the turmoil in their auras. This was a hell of a big hammer to keep them in line. Everyone had seen how tough the Kresh were. They needed our support.

"Now the subject is closed," I said. "If you want the support we have to offer, you will buy the guns and use them as they are intended. Or don't buy the guns at all and the status quo stays the same. We will help wherever and whenever we can. There are limited numbers and we are spread across the globe. The Source weapons were created to help level the playing field for the Human Race. Use them as such and we'll get along fine."

"If you insist on shooting one another, it won't be with my weapons. That's all I have to say."

I walked out of the room. There would be arguments and harsh words, I was sure. But they would toe the line or be left behind. We didn't have time to be warring amongst ourselves any more.

At least the worst they could do to each other with my guns was to use them as clubs on each other.

***

"You could have told us," Marco said. "It might not have made us worry so much and would've, definitely, made it easier for us to make our bosses feel better about it."

"In all honesty," I said. "I needed that scenario to play out so I could have this very example to use."

"But our boys wouldn't..."

"They did."

"What?!"

"There were five different countries that tried to use the Source weapons on other Humans. Only one was ballsy enough to want a refund."

There was a look of disgust on Polo's face.

"Our country tried," he said. "That bothers me more than I would like to think. I know we have enemies in our world that would see us destroyed. I expected it from them. I never expected to be the ones who fell short."

"I expected several to do it," I said, "but, honestly I am a little disappointed with the ones who did. You make sure the bosses know my threat is real. It would break my heart to walk out of America. I was born here and I love this country. But I have this world and fourteen others depending on us to do our jobs. I will do it."

"If it's any consolation, after they tried, they left it be," I said. "Some of the others went through thousands of the weapons before they gave up. They tried to pull the guns apart with the same result. They melted down. They tried to hack the signal and the guns melted down. The failsafe is there for a reason and it took as long to develop as the rest of the technology."

"You know someone will figure it out one of these days," Polo said. "They'll keep trying."

"True," I said, "but I hope we're done with this before they do. If our world is safe from the Kresh, then you can blow yourselves up if you want to. My job will be done by then."

"Let's hope they don't get it figured out by then," Marco said.

"Amen to that," Polo agreed.

"I wanted to put a Source weapon in the hands of every human on the planet," I said. "It would have been glorious, it's not really feasible, though."

"In a perfect world," Polo said, "it *would* have been an amazing thing to see."

"If they come into China, they'll see as close to that as they could come. There are over a billion people in China and their army has grown on an even bigger scale than America's," I said. "Gregor told me they have over a million people under arms and Warren tells me they have ordered enough weapons to arm it."

"Damn, that's a lot people." Polo said. "Our forces have grown like crazy but that's insane."

"They may not be the best trained troops but there are a lot of 'em. And the numbers are still growing. I think they've taken this war to heart."

"Here's to the hope that the Kresh meet several hundred thousand Source weapons at their first step on the planet," Marco said.

"Amen to that," Polo agreed.

Chapter 26

Kil'Sin'Deres had been fairly close in his estimate. He had said within three months. The first attack happened three months and six days after we had gotten word from the other world.

It happened on the day I made my mother a Mageguard.

"Ya finally decided to do it?" I asked.

"Yeah." she said. "The lure of being able to throw Kharl through a wall is just too much. I have to."

"I don't blame ya," I said, "though sadly, I can't throw him through a wall. We could always enlist Paige."

"Now wouldn't that be something to see," she said. "That tiny little thing shaking him like a rag doll."

"I'd pay real money to see that," I said with a laugh.

"I know this isn't a scheduled day for this," she said, "so do you want to wait until Sunday?"

"Now's fine, Mom," I said. "We told the ones on duty that we would be doin' this. That should be fine."

"Maybe you would like to do two," a voice behind me said.

I turned to find Dietrich. With him were Kharl, Prada, Lyrica, Mattie, Trent, and Rostov.

"I figured with just one, I wouldn't need supports," I said.

"You probably will need support to Pull hard enough to stretch his Stream, though," Lyrica said, pointing at Dietrich.

"You're probably right," I said.

Dietrich was six hundred and fifty years old and his Soulstream was already big enough to Pull through. Age strengthens the Stream and six centuries had made his look like steel cable. What I would have to Pull through that to make it grow would be extreme.

"Ok, we'll do Mom's first then the geezer."

"Geezer?" Dietrich rumbled.

"Anyone as old as you is automatically in the geezer category," Trent said. "Sorry no way to escape that."

"What happened to the term, 'respect your elders'?"

"Oh, don't get me wrong," Trent said, "I respect anyone that reaches geezer status. But, if there's a doubt, there's one person who can't even be denied as 'Geezer'. It would have to be the father of a guy that has reached geezer status, himself. There's no way to argue the point that this father we are speaking of could be anything less than an 'Old Geezer'."

"May even be considered ancient," I said, "I mean, you're old enough to have passed any sort of regular Geezer status."

"Maybe he needs a Title," Lyrica said, "say First Geezer, or something like that."

"All in capital letters," Rostov added.

"I at least expected the Russian to be on my side."

"We set great store in our ancestry," Rostov said, "We honor our eldest with Titles. FIRST GEEZER should be worn with pride."

"We can get a t-shirt for him and everything," Trent said.

"They'll have to make it out of a tent," I said.

"Probably cost a fortune," Prada said, "Lucky we got an international arms dealer who can afford it."

"You've been looking for a reason to use that term in a conversation for a week," Mattie said.

"How often do ya get to say that in regular conversation? Really?"

"True enough," I said, "And I'll gladly pay for a t-shirt for the FIRST GEEZER."

"Dear God," Dietrich said, "Can we just get this done before I have to shoot myself in the head."

"Alright, alright," I said.

"First we'll work with..."

"If you call me Geezer, I'll stab you."

"...the beautiful young lady," I continued.

Much like most of the others, Mom's ascension went just fine. She ended up with a stream about the same size as Kharl's.

Dietrich's was a different story.

He formed the tube for the power to flow from and, with several supports, I Pulled through it. After seeing that he steered it out the tube into the sky, I Pulled harder.

Fire poured through his stream into the sky, but the stream remained the same. I Pulled with more will and I felt power begin to flow from my supporters. His Stream may have grown an inch.

Lyrica stepped up beside me and our hands joined. We Pulled together and there was a massive explosion of power into the sky. As we Pulled, his stream grew little by little. I looked down into the Source. I could see something deep down inside there and I started to reach for it.

"Don't even think about it," Lyrica said, "'cause we aren't touching that. Ever."

I stopped myself from reaching for it and we just kept Pulling until Dietrich's Soulstream had grown to about the size of mine. The amount of power it would take to swell it further would be immense. It took ten minutes of steady Pulling from both of us to do that much.

"Damnit, man!" I said when we stopped and released the residual power into the sky, "What the hell is that thing made of?"

"The despair of my enemies and the lamentations of their women," he said.

"He is your father," Kyra said to Kharl.

"We don't call him the First Geezer for nothing," Kharl answered.

I laughed and turned to see a great deal of excitement going on back toward the base. People were running all over the place.

"That doesn't look good," I said.

"Not in the least," Kharl said, "so let's go see what's goin' on."

"Sorry, you two," I said, "there's no time to get you acclimated. I think the war may be starting."

"Go," Kyra said, "and we'll be along shortly once we get used to the power levels."

I nodded and launched myself toward the base with a crunch as the ground cracked where I had jumped from.

As I landed, Kharl passed me, "Damn grasshopper."

I stopped the first person I came across, a National Guardsman.

"What's happened?"

"They're hittin' all over Europe, Sir," he said, "currently London, Berlin, Paris, Prague, and a bunch more. It's on the news and we're getting ready in case they come here."

I didn't think they would be comin' through our Gate again any time soon, but we would have to prepare for it just in case.

"Alright, get back to it, then," I said. "We need to get to Paige's office or Marco and Polo's. Kharl, get your Jaeghernauts together and ready if the Gate opens."

"Will do. I got some new guys after Daphne took off to Edinburgh, last month. She's building another squadron of Juggs over there."

"Good, we need all of 'em we can get."

"The rest of ya," I said, "go gather your squads. More than likely, we're airborne within the next couple of hours. We gotta get over there before they open one of those Great Gates if we can."

"You Got it Boss," Prada said. "We'll be ready."

"Do you intend to leave me behind again?" Lyrica asked.

"Hell no," I said, "so you guys get ready to go too."

Mattie had what I think most would consider a feral grin on her face. She wasn't out in the middle of the last two major actions and she looked forward to this one."

"Bloodthirsty women," I muttered.

"You can say that again," Trent said before following behind the two of them.

I headed for Marco and Polo's building, it was closer than Paige's office. Turns out it was just as well. Paige and Gregor were both there too.

"They're all over Europe," Paige said, "The response is good from our Academy but the death toll is going to be enormous."

"They did one city at a time here," Gregor said, "It looks like these are on blitz runs. Regular Kresh and soldiers, mostly."

"Still, it's ugly," Polo said.

"I need to get over there," I said.

"Can we risk them not coming here and send our primary weapon over there?" Marco asked.

"They're not comin' here," I said, "and if they do we have so many weapons waitin' for 'em, it would be a slaughter. I need to be where they come out. And it's gonna be over there somewhere."

"Ok," Paige said, "and how many do you want to take with you?"

"I'll take my whole squad," I said, "and two others. Should take three planes. If you wanna send some AC130s along with us, I think we could spare a few here. I know we can use 'em over there. Once the Gate opens and they give us a target, we can bring more of 'em."

"Done and done," Marco said. "Go get 'em, Colin. We'll hold the Gate. Nothin' will get through here."

"Alright," I said, "I'm headin' out as soon as we can get our team ready."

"The Paris attack has been put down," Came a voice from the hallway.

"That's some good news. That was quick, too."

"Find out what they did to end it so quickly," I said, "and maybe we can use it in some of the others."

I strode out the door and as soon as I was clear of the office, took off at seventy miles per hour toward the Armory. I needed to suit up.

I stopped by my office to tell my staff what was happening and found a present sitting on my desk.

I looked around quickly and opened it. Inside a wooden box was a pair of swords. They were modeled after our short swords we used in the Guard. But they were of a quality that blew ours away.

Under them was a note.

I love you.
She knows me so well.

Chapter 27

The plane was loud but the video on Brighton's tablet didn't have any sound anyway. We watched a quiet day in Paris turn into a vision of Hell.

The video taker had been facing directly toward the spot where the Gate opened. Kresh poured through in a flood.

The guy turned and ran so we lost sight of the Kresh for a few minutes as he sprinted down the street.

Suddenly, something caught his eye and he faced the camera toward a restaurant where a woman had exited the door with flames rolling across her body. She wore a form fitting black dress and high heels.

"Isn't that..."

"Yep, Daphne Cavanaugh," I said.

"Oh," Prada said, "they definitely shouldn't have interrupted her date. Now they're in trouble."

She strode past the man with the camera and the camera shook as she began firing discs of Soulfire into the packed throngs of Kresh pouring down the street.

We saw her discs clear the running Humans and ripped holes in the ranks of the pursuing Kresh. I could see the intensity of the fire rolling across Daphne growing.

"She can't keep doing that," Adaya said, "or she'll burn out."

As if she had heard the words, Daphne stopped firing her launcher. She reached down and removed her heels and buckled them together and laid them across her shoulder.

"Never just throw away a set of five inch stilettos," Mattie said, "'cause those are beautiful."

"Sure Mattie," Trent said.

Daphne charged into the horde of Soldiers and they seemed to explode as anything that came within reach of her was ripped apart.

The guy with the camera had lost all interest in running away. He was mesmerized by the sight in front of him.

Daphne went down under a pile of soldiers.

"Oh God," Prada said.

"Nope," I said, "wait for it."

The pile exploded in every direction as Daphne burst out of it like some Greek goddess. She was bloody and wounded, not to mention nearly naked. She still had her shoes.

"Perhaps not the best time to have worn a thong," Prada said.

The camera was pointed at her but the gate was plainly visible in front of her. She continued her rampage through the soldiers and literally went through a Wraith that had come out of the Gate.

She was right up against the Gate when a Kresh'Ma'Nar strode through the portal. It was moving fast and was past her in an instant. But

Daphne is a Mage with a twenty inch Soulstream. She was on it before it even knew she was there.

She was up its back with her shoes in her hand. They glowed with Soulfire as she imbued her five inch heels.

"Ohhh!" I heard Mattie as Daphne slammed her fiery heels into both of the Demon Mage's ears.

The heels pierced its brain and it fell forward onto its face. What Kresh were left turned from their victims, and you could see the roars as they charged back toward her.

She screamed something I expect was rather mean at them and met them half way.

She tore them apart. The gate closed.

The camera stayed on her as she limped over to the fallen Mage and bent down. She calmly pulled her shoes from its ears and buckled them back together.

Someone came out of the crowd with a long jacket which he handed to her. She put it on and thanked the man.

"Don't look so disappointed," Prada said.

"Men," Adaya said.

"She saved the shoes," Mattie said.

"She saved a lot of people," Brighton said.

"Well, that too," Mattie said.

***

We landed in England and refueled again. The flight seemed to take forever but it was necessary. We needed the planes over here to use. Everything we had over here was already in use. The Great Gate had opened in Kenya, Africa. Before we could take off again there was a man brought to me from the African Academy.

"Sir I was ordered to report directly to you."

I could see the bitterness inside of him. Something had happened that had been rough for him.

"Just think about what happened and I'll watch it."

His thoughts returned to the previous days. His thoughts returned to his posting at Nanyuki. To his Mage Captain, Malcolm Hendrix. I remembered Malcolm. I had made him a Mage some time back. A powerful Mage at that.

"Sir, there's no way you can stop that with thirty Mages. We all have to go!"

"No, Sovas, your job is to get as many women and children in the planes and get them out of here. You, personally will be on the first plane. You will report directly to Colin Rourke. Tell him what happened here. You tell him we held them as long as we could. Most importantly, you tell him where this Gate is so he can drop Hell on it. Do you understand?"

"Yes, Sir," Sovas answered.

I could feel the misery as this man had watched thirty Mages run South toward what he could feel as the most Demons he had ever felt in the same spot before. The pictures had just come in from the drones that were sent South. They had been disheartening. There were hundreds of thousands of Kresh already out and running. They poured through in rivers.

Sovas followed orders and gave the commands to remove all women and children from the city that they could fit in any plane available. He was on the first and he looked back with tears in his eyes as he saw the massive explosion to the south. He knew he was watching the deaths of many of his brothers. He longed to be there with them.

I placed my hand on his shoulder, "You'll be with me when we get there, Sovas. I swear it."

"They held them long enough to get ten planes out of Nanyuki."

"We'll make them pay," I said with a fire burning inside me that would not be pushed down. Those men had ran straight into that Hell to save as many as they could and I would not let them die in vain.

"Change of plans," I said, "We're goin' for the Gate and we're goin' to close it, one way or another."

"Yes Sir," said our pilot, "I'll call it in."

I went back to my seat alongside the right wall of the plane. My rage was clawing to get free and I needed to center myself. What had happened in Nanyuki is what I would expect of any Mage Captain. I hated that we had lost those men, but they died as Soulguards die. With honor and protecting those that cannot protect themselves. The problem with that situation was that we would all die piecemeal if we couldn't get our forces together. None of the garrison in Nanyuki had survived except Sovas. It would haunt him, I'm sure but we would give the man a chance to see his brothers avenged. It's the best I can do for him.

"We have com signal from the Academy in Africa, Sir," the pilot said over my coms.

"Patch me in," I said.

"This is Rourke," I said after I heard the click in my coms.

"We've loaded all the civilians from the Academy, Sir," Ekene Dakarai said.

Dakarai was the Dean of the African Academy and a powerful Mage in his own right but I knew they couldn't stand up to the wave of Kresh coming up through Kenya straight toward them.

We couldn't face them like this or they would destroy our world. The Source weapons weren't plentiful enough in one place yet.

"I need you to pull out, Dakarai," I said. "We have to hit 'em on a unified front. Forces are buildin' up in Cairo to meet the bastards."

"It's too late for that, Sir," he said with a shake of his head. "We've sent all the civilians out with the planes and they're too close."

"Then you hit the hills," I said. "Don't waste men on a frontal assault. Guerilla tactics only, Dakarai. We'll send planes down to get you as soon as we can. But you have to stay alive so we can fight these bastards together. You hear me?"

"Yes Sir, we'll do our best," he said.

"I know you will," I said, "you're Soulguard."

"Yes Sir, Dakarai out."

"Good luck and Godspeed, Dakarai."

I turned to Rostov, "Get word back to base, we need planes to go after those men. As soon as we hit that gate, we go join them in Cairo, as well."

He nodded and headed for the cockpit.

The rage was clawing its way out again as I thought of all the people dying down there. Several of the Mageguards were staring at me. My rage was leaking and they could all feel it. Some of these men had only fought in training alongside me and they didn't know the depths of the rage.

What I had just ordered Dakarai to do would not sit well with them but we have to pull everything together for a unified attack. If there's one thing I have learned in the last few days, I can't be everywhere I'm needed and it eats at me. I need to be at the Gate, I need to be in Cairo, I needed to be in Berlin, London, Prague, Rome and a dozen other cities in Europe.

The small gates were opening all over Europe to spread our forces and they were doing a swell job of it. The forces that were on their way to Cairo consisted of military units from ten different countries.

So far, the Kresh had followed a fairly straight line up through Kenya, straight toward Egypt and the small land bridge that allowed access to the Middle Eastern countries and Europe.

Europe seemed to be the main target, though. The gates seemed focused there. But the death toll in North Eastern Africa was going to be horrendous. Evacuation of the countries between Kenya and Egypt were underway but that was a lot of damn people.

The problem was that the gate kept spewing Kresh even as the others poured through the country.

We had three planes full of Mages and Mageguards and we would close the gate. If we could get to a place where we could reload on the plane, we would. Otherwise, we would fight our way out of Africa.

It was scary to know that my desire to use the second option was far stronger than the desire to use the first. Unfettered, the beast inside me could bath in the blood of our enemies.

I looked up to find some disturbing expressions around me, and I sensed the feelings behind them. They feared what they were seeing and feeling as my emotions were projecting outward.

It might have had something to do with the vicious grin that was on my face as I thought of the slaughter to come.

Chapter 28

"Sir there's something you need to see," Rostov said as he rested his hand on my shoulder.

I jerked around with fires burning in my eyes. I could feel the bastards and my rage was almost unbearable.

I beat it back down and shook my head to clear it.

"What is it, Alexei?"

"There's a detachment of Marines down below. A force of Kresh has split off and headed toward a small city. Perhaps ten thousand. We'll be overhead in less than ten minutes."

I clicked my coms for the pilot, "Have we got enough fuel to land and take back off and still reach the gate?"

"Yes Sir."

"Good," I said, "then tell the others we're gonna hit that force hard."

"Yes Sir."

I got up and headed toward where Prada sat with her squad.

"We're hittin' a force in less than ten," I said. "I want you, Lyr, Trent, and Mattie to hit the ground and protect the marines down there. Your squad will be with me."

"Got it," she said and headed back toward the opening doors on the back of the plane.

"Trent!"

"Boss?" he said from the right.

"You have one job," I said.

"Roger."

"Throw Prada out of the plane and follow her."

"Yes Sir!" he said with a grin.

Prada's head jerked around at the order but it was too late. He slammed into her and both went out the door.

Mattie was laughing as she ran past, "I love this job!"

"Be careful, Love," Lyrica said as she followed them out the door.

"All right, boys and girls!" I yelled, "let's show the bastards what Hell looks like! Rostov! Brighton! You're with me! Combat drop."

***

"There's a lot of the bastards down there, Sir," Corporal Santos whispered.

"You got that right, Santos," Sergeant Hicks whispered, "Get on that radio and call in a strike. There's no way we can do anything with that many."

Hicks was peering over the ridgeline and what he was seeing left a large hollow pit in his stomach. The Kresh poured across the valley below like a swarm of locusts. There were so many, he couldn't see the ground below them. He also knew that they were moving toward the small town down on the plains below the ridges. It was several miles away but it would be impossible to evacuate in time. These things could run like the wind.

"Sir, they say we have ordinance incoming already," Corporal Santos slid in beside him.

"We haven't lazed the target yet."

"Different ordinance, Sir."

Hicks looked upward as he heard the roar of the engines. Three C-130s swept through the sky above them and forms began launching from the rear of the planes. It looked like clusters of men and women floated toward the ground. One of the clusters rocketed toward the ground.

Hicks winced as he figured whatever these guys use as parachutes must have failed. About five hundred feet up, that cluster seemed to explode. Hicks felt his skin crawl and his teeth seemed to vibrate. It ached all the way to his core. This had been described to him before by some of the men he'd served with. They had served with Soulguard before and this was what it felt like when their Mages did their thing.

He watched as the whole cluster slowed and slammed into the ground right in the center of that horde. A huge plume of dust shot skyward and fire exploded outward from the impact.

"He's always doin' that," Hicks heard a voice from behind him.

Hicks spun around to find two women stepping from the shadows of the trees behind them. More forms stepped out as well and Hicks found himself facing a pretty woman with brown hair. She wore black body armor and he could see the hilts of a pair of swords crossed on her back.

"My, aren't you a pretty one," she said.

She moved so fast, he just saw a blur. She was standing right in front of him. Her finger ran along the scar that led from his right cheekbone, down across his jaw.

"Got a thing for scars, handsome," she said with a smile, "I got a few myself. Maybe I'll show em to you sometime."

"Damn, Andrea," the other woman interrupted, "horde of Demons, over the ridge, remember?"

"Yeah, yeah," Andrea said with a wink at Hicks. "Later, big boy."

The two women walked right past the squad with their two followers right behind them.

"All right," the second woman said, "shall we distract them till everyone gets on the ground?"

"Looks like he already distracted them quite well, Lyrica."

"Why should he get all the fun?" Lyrica returned. "He always sends me off to the side. I'm getting a little tired of that."

"Ma'am," Hicks said, "looks like they've seen you already, they're headed this way."

Both women looked toward the horde that rolled toward them.

"Nice," the one named Lyrica said. She clapped her hands and Hicks cringed as he thought of what it looked like.

Friggin' cheerleaders, he thought.

"You know," one of their followers said, "she's getting as bad as him."

He was a six foot tall man that looked at home in his armor. The tiny woman beside him looked out of place until Hicks saw her eyes. There was a fire burning inside them that sent chills down his spine.

"Not quite," she said, "she just wants..."

She spied the young woman bouncing and clapping her hands.

"On second thought, you're probably right."

"Oh my God! Did you just say I was right?"

Hicks had seen a lot of things in his career as a soldier, but he was having trouble wrapping his mind around the situation that was unfolding around him. A flood of Kresh were pouring toward them and he was surrounded by kids.

He went to one knee and raised his rifle toward the approaching Kresh and moments before he would pull the trigger they slammed to a stop against an invisible wall. He motioned for his men to hold their fire.

"He said to shield these guys," Lyrica said. "He didn't say we couldn't attack too."

"I think that was sort of unspoken, honey," Andrea answered.

"But I don't see why we can't do both," Lyrica said. "He didn't specifically say not to. And there's no injured people so I don't see the harm in it."

"The plan is for him to draw them to him," the big man said. "If you blast a shitload of 'em, it may interfer with his game plan."

"Of course, you're gonna take his side," Lyrica said. "Damn these things are loud."

The roars and screams from the Kresh pounding on her shield was getting louder.

Hicks was still a bit dazed as he watched the girl argue with her cohorts. His mouth dropped open when the girl snarled and turned back toward the roaring horde.

"Shut up!" she yelled and he felt something.

It looked like every Kresh within a hundred feet of the shield just fell in pieces. Like a razor blade had ripped through them, they fell in parts with explosions of blood.

"The blade seems to work well," the tiny woman said with one eyebrow raised.

"Thanks Mattie," Lyrica said with a smile, "At least Colin will be glad we tested that."

The center of the horde seemed to explode down in the valley and Hicks felt the ache in his teeth again.

"Looks like they pissed him off," Andrea said. "I bet he melts his swords again."

"He better not!" Lyrica said. "He has the ones I got for him. If he melts those, I'm gonna kick his ass!"

"Oh yeah," Mattie said, "there they go! Sorry, girl, those blades are toast. You see that Trent?"

"Yep, they're slag. Sorry Lyr."

"Son of a..."

"You gotta learn, babe," Andrea said. "You can't give him stuff to fight with and expect him not to break it."

"Next time he's just getting friggin' shoes."

"He has no respect for shoes, Lyrica, honey," Mattie said. "The first day I met him he dropped a Demon head on mine."

"Really?"

"Yeah, I had to burn them."

"How could he do that to shoes?" Lyrica asked. "Shoes are, like, sacred."

"Women," Trent turned to Hicks. "She has a hundred pairs of shoes, and she's bitchin about one pair. And it was like fifteen years ago. They never just forgive and forget. If I made as many mistakes as our boss does I'd be afraid to even talk to a woman. But I'm just about flawless so I don't have to worry about it like..."

"Flawless!? That's a joke," Mattie interrupted. "The only reason you don't have anyone trying to beat you to death is because you're so pretty, and everyone knows you're retarded so they make exceptions."

"You didn't act like I was retarded last night. You seemed pretty hap... ungh!"

The tiny woman had moved so fast Hicks hadn't even seen her move. The big man nearly doubled over.

"I'm about to stop making exceptions, Mister."

The Kresh were back at the shield and roaring. Then something happened down in the valley and every one of them turned away. They roared in unison and charged back into the valley.

"Oh, that got their attention," Andrea said. "You think he'll Alpha?"

"I doubt it," Lyrica said, "he likes to use the hands on approach. But there's always the chance he will."

She paused and cocked her head a little to the side.

"Looks like I was wrong," Lyrica said. "Sereno just shielded them up. He's gonna Alpha."

"Jesus Christ!" Corporal Santos said beside Hicks as the whole world seemed to shake around them.

"Oh! That's gonna leave a mark," Trent said with a chuckle as they watched the whole valley engulfed in flame.

Hicks was awestruck. These Soulguards were amazing. I wish we had a million of 'em, he thought.

The next instant the woman he'd seen first was standing directly in front of him.

"I'm Andrea Prada, Beautiful," she said and stretched her hand out, "and what I want to know is, do you have any plans for the weekend? I'd say tonight but we have to go stomp on a giant Gate."

Chapter 29

"She's gonna kill me," I said as we walked toward the group on the hill ahead of us.

"Maybe she doesn't know those were the ones she had made for you," Adaya said.

"You honestly believe that?" I asked.

"Not for a second," she said with a laugh, "You're in trouble."

"I was lookin' at 'em on the plane, and forgot to swap 'em back out before we jumped," I said.

"Don't whine," Reyna said, "it's so not befitting of the second in command of the Soulguard."

She laughed.

"What is it with women? You learn to tie a knot in your Soulstream and you get plain vicious."

"The female of the species is much deadlier than the male," Len Yueh said. "Haven't you ever heard that? It is fact."

"I think they're all just crazy," Cristof said. "Did you know I read that twenty five percent of women are on some sort of medication for psychological balancing?"

"Bloody Hell," Stone said, "guess that means seventy five percent of them are running around untreated!"

"Men," Adaya said sadly.

"Nothing you can really do with them," Reyna said.

Lyrica, Mattie and Trent were standing in front of the group of Marines but Prada was busy hitting on the Sergeant. Lyrica was giving me the look and I knew it would be trouble later. I winced and walked over to save the Sergeant.

"Sergeant," I said, "I'm Colin Rourke and this is my motley crew. They told me you guys got hung up down here before we left the plane. If you don't mind a little detour, you can hitch a ride back with us."

"We'd love to get a ride, Sir," he said. "What sort of detour did you have in mind?"

"We're goin' down to Kenya and close that Gate. Then we're gonna kill everything in the area that walks on two legs and ain't Human."

"I'm gonna say that sounds fun," he said. "My name's Hicks, this is Corporal Santos."

I nodded toward the Corporal with the radio.

"Get 'em ready, Santos."

"Sir"

Santos turned back toward the squad of Marines, spouting orders.

A moment later a man came from the forest behind the group. He held a huge sniper rifle.

"What took ya so long, Corn?" Hicks asked.

"Had a ring side seat for the show up on that bluff, Sir. Hated to leave the box seats."

"Get ready to move out. We're goin' to Kenya."

"Isn't that where the Gate opened?"

"Yep."

"Ooo-rah!"

I love Marines.

Corn turned and joined his fellows.

"Corn?" I said to Hicks.

"That's what we all call him," He said, "you don't even wanna know why. Trust me."

"I don't doubt that for a second," I said.

I turned and went back to see if Lyrica was gonna kill me now or later.

"I'm sorry, Baby," I said, "I didn't even realize those were the swords I had until after I jumped and it was too late."

"Um Hm," she said, "and that's why I can't buy you pretty things. Also I want to know why you always send me off to the side."

"Everyone needs a reserve force to pull their asses out of the fire if it all goes south."

"It sounds reasonable except for the fact, I can tell you're lying. But I'll let it go this time."

She kissed me and we turned back to find four women spaced behind us.

"Just in case she wanted help when she kicked your ass," Prada said. "Besides, I keep getting thrown out of planes, and I think ya get a lot more pleasure out of it than ya should."

"Damn bloodthirsty women," I muttered.

"I think *all* of ours are running around untreated," Stone said sadly.

"Yes," Rostov said, "we didn't even get our twenty five percent."

"Just for something to think about," Brighton said, "if you count the Mageguards and

Mages, both, the women in this Motley crew actually outnumber us. Just a little food for thought before you say anything else on the subject."

He was right. Out of the Three hundred and forty Soulguards that were in the three planes, close to two hundred of them were women.

"So what you are saying is there are two hundred of them running around, untreated, right here?" Rostov asked.

"Well, yeah."

There were a lot of women with that "look" standing around us.

"Ahem," I coughed, "let's go find our planes."

"Good idea," Rostov said.

"Everybody move out!" I said. "The planes are down on the other side of the town. Small airstrip."

"Grab a Marine and we'll take it at a run."

Mattie grabbed the sniper who yelped as she slung him over her shoulder.

"Your hands go anywhere they shouldn't and you'll be creamed Corn. Got it?"

"Both hands on my rifle, Ma'am!"

I laughed.

Prada, of course, grabbed Hicks.

"Honey, your hands can go anywhere they want," she said.

We took off at high speed across the ridgeline toward town and reached the airstrip in less than fifteen minutes.

The small strip had a fueling station, and our pilots had topped off our tanks. The guy at the airstrip said it was free after we had just saved his town.

We were airborne once more in a short time and back on the way toward Kenya. There were a couple of small wounds and Lyrica made her rounds to heal them. Most of the wounds were superficial and Mages heal fast, anyway. But the added help she could give wasn't turned down by any.

"A Medic?" Hicks asked, "but she's so young."

"She's been doin' hands-on trainin' for the last few years at the Hospital in Wichita or the one in Montana," I said.

"We could use a Medic like that. It's like the games I used to play. We always wanted a healer in our groups."

"You're a Gamer?" I asked.

"Before I joined."

"I used to play some in our down time before the Kresh decided they had to kill us all. I always played a tank."

"Me too," he said.

"Come to find out, I ended up as a real tank. I go out into the middle and get their attention and then we can all bring down the fire."

"You seem to do it well enough," he said with a chuckle. "I saw the footage from both First and Second Kansas. They used to call the sort of guy you are a Berserker in the old days."

"There's something inside me," I said, "and when it comes out, well, you've seen the footage."

Sergeant Hicks was a perceptive guy. He could see the shame I felt over what I become sometimes.

"A world at peace can be ashamed of the guys like us, Mister Rourke," he said. "A world at war will cherish us. There's no shame in what happened in Kansas. They came here to commit genocide on our race. Our job is to show them it will cost them too much. Our job is to be the meanest sons of bitches on the planet. We'll do what it takes to get the job done. That's all I see you've been doing. There's no shame in that."

"Just doin' the job, huh?" I asked.

"Damn right," he said, "and doing it well."

Chapter 30

I could feel the gate below us and my rage was bleeding through my walls. It's so hard to keep it beat down as we wait to be able to attack. The hours and hours of riding in the plane had been torturous. Our little side trip helped a lot but the wait was almost over.

I could see the Souls below us as we made a circle of the Gate. They were pouring through the Gate as fast as they could run through it. And that was pretty fast. The newcomers pushing the ones ahead of them.

"If we hit out right in front of the Gate, they'll keep pourin' through," I said.

"What if we hit about a quarter mile up the stream and cause a traffic jam?" asked Brighton.

"That may be workable," I said, "and if we get 'em all jammed up at the Gate, we can drop an Alpha on 'em. Then we gotta close the Gate. We used a contraption I built to do it last time and it worked, so that may be the best way to go. I'd love to study the damn thing from this side, but we don't have time."

"I don't see a Farrara'Ti down there," Lyrica said. "It must either be through already or still on the other side."

"One of our prime objectives is to find that bastard and kill it. Don't go after it if you find it. I saw the power at Kil'Sin'Deres' disposal. You don't wanna tangle with that. Leave him to me. That goes for you too, Lyr. The safest way to kill one of 'em is to rip it's Soul out. I'm the only one who can do that."

She nodded, "Use that skill sparingly, my love, as it doesn't come without its price."

"That I know," I said, "but it's one I have to pay. Those bastards are tough."

"What about the Mark?" Rostov asked.

"I don't have the juice to take this guy without the backup of the Shak'Tar or another group of Kresh. Plus the Mark is indiscriminate. It would Mark all of you, as well as the Kresh. It's not something we can use."

He nodded.

I clicked my coms, "Move us about a quarter mile north and keep the altitude. We'll jump from there. The nearest airstrip I know of is the Academy. We'll rejoin you there if we can."

"Roger."

"Hicks, I need your guys to set up when the planes land. Keep our guys safe and if it gets hairy, make 'em leave. We can come out on foot if we need to."

"Will do," he said.

"Alexei, Adaya, you're with Lyrica," I said, "Combat drop. Prada, Brighton, you're with me. Lyrica, I want you guys on the left side of that valley mouth. I'll be on the right. Juggernaut and come together. We'll create a landing zone for the rest."

"Got it." Lyrica said and headed for the rear of the plane.

"Keep her safe," I said to Trent and Mattie as they passed me.

"Will do," Trent said.

Mattie nodded as she went past. I knew they would be at her back and I wouldn't need to worry. They would never let anything get to her.

Prada and Brighton were at the rear of the plane when I got there and I pushed Prada out the door and Brighton laughed and followed. I was right behind them.

My adrenaline was spiking and my beast was at the gates. I focused on the ground below and the Kresh I was about to destroy. I formed the platform and my group formed up on it. We hit our chosen height and gave the signal. Prada and Brighton pulled and I snatched the power and added my own. The blast of power slowed our platform, the pressure pushing down on us. Then I signaled again and closed the portal on the feeder.

We landed with a crash amidst the charred forms of the Kresh that had been below us.

"Fire!" I ordered and Prada, Brighton and myself opened up with our disc launchers. Each of us faced a different direction so our discs blew a great hole in the center of the Kresh around us.

"Juggernauts!" I ordered and all of us opened the portals on our juggernaut armor.

The Juggernaut armor is a shield that incorporates most of a Mages Soulstream to feed. It is a large shield with blades along the sides that will demolish anything in its path. The front is sloped like the front guard of a train with blades along the top as well.

Each of the Mageguards is trained how to construct this shield as soon as they are ascended. It doesn't require a Pull and it is a devastating weapon.

We formed a V formation and launched ourselves forward, toward the center of the valley mouth we had aimed for.

I could see Lyrica's group hit across from us and erupt in fire. Then I hit the first of the Kresh and blood exploded around me from the multitude of blades I had placed on my Juggernaut shield. For large, compact groups of Kresh, the juggernaut shield is ideal. When they aren't as packed, Kresh can dodge around us.

What we ran through here, was a huge compacted group of Kresh. They resembled sausage after we had passed.

I still had to reign in the beast in me. This was important. When I could set it free it would be when we were hand to hand with the enemy. It would come soon enough.

"We meet in the middle," I said over the coms, "then Lyrica is goin' to raise a shield across the mouth of the valley."

"Roger," Lyrica said.

"Then we drop the sky on that Gate and all the Kresh around it. When I give the word, Reyna will raise a shield between us and the valley and we'll Alpha. Then we go for the Gate."

"Copy," Reyna returned.

"We've only got thirty Mages for the Alpha but, we'll do what we can. Need to work with some of the Mageguards after this to be able to do that Pull."

"Give me a minute and I'll whip out my notebook and write that down for ya," Prada said.

"Smart ass," I returned.

"You did throw me out of another plane."

"No, it was the same plane."

"We killing Kresh or doing a stand-up act for them?" Lyrica's voice interrupted, "Battle Com System."

I laughed as my shield slammed through the last of the Kresh between our converging groups.

Lyrica dropped her Juggernaut shield and raised another across the mouth of the valley.

Reyna dropped hers and raised another on the other side of our party. We slaughtered the few Kresh that were inside the perimeter.

"Alright," I said, "Ten supports. Code Alpha."

Thirty Mages Pulled and steered the power upwards where I snatched it. Power flowed through ten streams into me as my body balanced the power usage.

I turned the fire in the sky into the circling pattern for a good thirty seconds. Then I slammed the whole roiling mass into the ground with the Gate as the center of the inferno.

"Cease."

The power stopped pouring into the sky and I threw the rest of what was already there at the Gate.

When the smoke and mist cleared we could see very few living Kresh near the Gate but the valley was still crawling with them. There wasn't anything coming through the Gate at the moment. The blast of fire must have gone through the Gate when I dropped it.

"Time to clean 'em out and go for the gate," I said. "Lyr, keep the shield up and Prada, your squad is guarding her. The rest, split into two groups. One with me, one with Rostov. Rostov on the left. I'll take the right. Kill everything that moves and ain't Human."

Rostov headed left and I headed right. Reyna dropped her shield and I let the beast out of its cage.

When I let it out, it scares me because I love it so. Rage floods my mind and my whole being is consumed for a moment. I push past it to a clarity I don't see that often. It's like I'm riding this monstrous beast. I can barely control it and sometimes I lose control altogether.

The beast consists of two things most of the time. Rage and Power. I used them both as I launched myself into the horde of Kresh and Kresh'Far.

My inhuman roar echoed across the valley, and I ripped anything within my reach apart. I Pulled and fire exploded in front of me. The ones who followed me spread out into a v formation and we rolled over the Kresh. Discs exploded forward from any of the Mages and the Mageguards waded into the horde and tore them to shreds.

It was different from the last invasion in Kansas. There we faced them with Soulguards. Mageguards, well, they're another thing. They fight as Guards fight but they have the strength and speed of Mages. There isn't much that can stand up to an onslaught like that and this small valley full of Kresh wasn't one of them.

I saw a black shield come through the Gate and my beast roared, victoriously. Could we be this lucky? I turned and charged toward the Gate. The shielded figure stopped and surveyed the area. I felt his mental commands and the Gate closed.

He should have backed through it, first.

I ripped his shield apart and was inside in a fraction of a second. I saw his aura as surprise flooded it at the ease I had gotten to him. He started to Pull but my discs started hammering into his chest. He was a strong Kresh'Ma'Nar, but my discs ripped through his chest in an explosion of fire, blood and ash.

The shield was gone and all of the remaining Kresh charged toward me. I stood and waited.

Most of them were picked off by the Mageguards as the charged toward me. One lone Kresh'Far made it through and I seized it by the throat. It froze as I looked into its mind and it felt the strength of the mental grip I put on it.

It was six and a half feet tall and I had seized it and slammed it to the ground. I stared deep into its eyes.

"Tell them Rash'Tor'Ri is coming for them. Tell them to run as fast as they can. I come to devour their Souls."

I threw the Kresh'Far toward the shielded mouth of the valley. The Kresh on the other side were long gone toward the north.

"Drop the shield," I said over coms.

As the Kresh'Far landed, he looked back at me with fear in his Soul. He ran north past Lyrica and her group.

Chapter 31

"Apparently," I said, "my little trip over to Kresh has made 'em a little skittish."

We stood near where the Gate had been.

"Accordin' to what I saw in its mind," I said, "they came here because I was in Kansas. They're worried I'll go back and kill more Farrara'Ti. That was why that Ma'Nar ordered the Gate closed."

"But you're such a likable chap," Stone said.

"He does tend to break stuff," Prada said.

"You can't buy him anything pretty," Lyrica said.

"I'm right here."

"He flies off the handle at a moment's notice," Trent added.

"Always running around screaming," Reyna said.

"Leaving Graffiti on walls," Adaya said.

"Right here, people."

"Killing, I guess you'd call them, leaders of state," Mattie said.

I just walked away. As I looked around the small river valley, I had an idea. The sides of the valley were far enough away from the Gate that we'd never get enough power to blow the sides in to cover the Gate.

"How deep do ya think this valley is?" I asked.

"Fifty, maybe sixty feet," Brighton answered.

"So what if we put a dam on the mouth and let this Gate be at the bottom of a lake?"

"They have to have some sort of system to let them know the Gate is blocked," Lyrica said, "so it might just work."

"So how do you make a dam that will hold?" Rostov asked.

"We call Jack," I said, "He's an engineer. Who's got the sat phone?"

As everybody pointed at each other, I sighed.

"Did we leave it on the plane?"

Silence.

"Damnit."

"We'll just do the best we can," Lyrica said, "Then after we kill the rest of the bastards, we'll come back and make sure it holds."

"I guess so. Let's get to it then."

We jogged toward the mouth of the valley. The opening was about a thousand feet across.

"Lyr, you build a wall and plant it deep, maybe forty feet. I'll build a sloped back and do the same. Then we'll connect em."

"Sounds good."

It took a little while. But once we planted the walls, we met in the middle with the feeders.

"I sure hope this doesn't blow up," I said, looking at the parts we had planted in the ground.

"It's a construct, it won't blow up," Reyna said. "What blew up was when you filled the empty spot between the shield walls with the Source. Let's not do that here."

Everyone backed up and raised their personal shields anyway.

"You first," I said to Lyrica, "and then me."

She pushed her twenty four inch feeder into the ground and the Source poured into the construct. I watched as the dam took shape and as the power poured up the feeder I was connected to, I pushed it into the Source and cut my connection. The power fluctuated and the construct was finished.

The water from the river began to whitewater where it hit the shield and I could already see it start to rise.

"Let's hope it's strong enough to do the job," I said, "Now it's time to keep a promise I made that Kresh. We pursue and kill any that we can get ahold of. Maybe we can keep 'em movin' fast enough to miss some people."

"If we're lucky," Trent said, "more than likely, they'll all turn around and dogpile us."

"Target rich environment," I said.

"You may be a nutbar," Trent said, "but I kinda like ya. So let's get on with it."

"Damn right."

We started north at a run. Lyrica ran right by my side, and I was remembering days spent running through the hills of Montana. I think that may have been when I really fell in love with her. I'm not certain. I just knew at some point that I could not imagine a life without her. It really came to the fore when I had thought the Shak'Tar had killed her. I was deep in thought and I almost missed the group of Soulguards coming from the east, toward us.

"Halt," I said over coms and our group slowed down and came to rest.

"What is it, boss?" Rostov asked.

"We've got company inbound," I said, "It looks like the group from the Academy. We'll wait here for 'em."

"They must have seen the ruckus at the Gate," Adaya said.

I Pulled and sent a fiery blast into the sky for them to home in on. Lyrica and I could see Souls. No one else I had ever met could do that.

The group turned their path toward us. We didn't have to wait long before they cleared the hills and closed with us.

Ekene Dakarai stopped in front of me. I had never actually met him and he was tall. Nearly seven feet tall. He wasn't huge like Kharl, but tall like a basketball player. I had to look up at him.

"Rourke," he said with his huge hand outstretched.

"Good to meet ya, Dakarai," I said and shook hands.

"We saw the fireworks down at the Gate and figured it might be you," he said, "Malcolm has told us many stories of the Soullord since he came back."

"He was a good man," I said. "It saddened me to see him and his men fall."

"Me, as well," he said, "so what are your plans?"

"I intend to attack their rear and drive them north. Hopefully we can push 'em faster and they'll start missin' people. The countries above us are being evacuated for the most part but there will be people still there. Some wouldn't have left or were just plain missed. If we keep pushin' they may yet survive this."

"How do you know they will run?"

"Because every time we get within range, we're gonna drop the sky on 'em. They don't like that. If we get lucky we'll find the Farrara'Ti and really piss 'em off. If that happens, we run north and they follow. That's about as much planning as I have."

"Simple but it should be effective," he said.

"Fall in with us," I said. "We're makin' a stop at the Academy first and sending any wounded out with Lyrica on the planes. How many of your guys are hurt?"

"We have a camp in the hills over there," he said. "There are nearly a hundred wounded there and some of our men are wounded here but I couldn't get them to stay."

"Here's what we'll do," I said. "Lyr, I need you to take a couple of our squads and get those wounded to the planes at the Academy. We'll send some of Dakarai's wounded with you so you can find the camp. As soon as you can, do your thing. We need healthy warriors. Get 'em to Cairo and tell them what we're doin'."

"You be careful, down here," she said. "Who do you want me to take?"

"Take Reyna," I said, "she's got the best shield."

"Then you should keep her," Lyrica said, "you'll be fighting, and I won't. Use your head here, not your heart."

She was right. I wanted her protected and that was influencing my choices. I could use Reyna's Shield.

"If I might make a suggestion," Dakarai said, "my injured are mostly Guards. The Mages are harder to kill. Keep all of the Mages and send the Guards with her. What we are about to do is infinitely more dangerous for them."

"That would be the smartest thing," I said. "Ok, that's the plan. Round 'em up and let 'em all know. We're headin' north in ten minutes."

Lyrica moved close and we kissed. The whole world was gone for a moment. The war, the Kresh, all the worries.

We parted and it all came back.

Ten minutes later, I started running north with seventy three Mages and three hundred and ninety Mageguards. When we caught up with them there would be hell to pay, and my beast was in the forefront of my mind, reveling in the hunt.

I poured on the speed. There wasn't much risk of running off from the group, they were all Mage strength and we could run like the wind.

Chapter 32

We caught up to the rear of their forces as they crossed into Ethiopia.

"What do you suggest?" I asked Dakarai. "A Juggernaut run before an Alpha, or just drop an Alpha from nowhere on 'em?"

"It depends on what message you want to send," he said. "If you want to just kill them, Alpha. If you want them to know who did it, get up inside them and make it personal. I've been waiting for the chance to do that from the moment we evacuated the Academy, so my opinion may be biased."

"You're a man after my own heart, Dakarai," I said. "Let's do it. We want 'em to know who's back here so everyone get as personal as you can and lets rip 'em a new one."

"Yes Sir," Dakarai said with a savage grin.

"Juggernaut armor," I ordered over the com. "Form up in diamonds. We go in 'til I give the signal. If we see a Farrara'Ti, it's mine. Anything else is fair game. When I signal, we reverse course and return to the back of the pack. Then Reyna raises a shield and we go Alpha. Any questions?"

There was silence as everyone assumed diamond formations. Each formation had fifty men. Ten per side and one at each point. Then six Mages in the center who would be using launchers on anything that came within range. There were nine formations.

"Pick an entry point and hit it." I said.

I opened my juggernaut shield and began running toward the horde of Kresh before us, my rage boiling through my consciousness. As I slammed into the rear of the Kresh, I roared my battle cry and Lashed with the same.

RASH'TOR'RI! Ripped through their minds and the area in front of me erupted in blood as my shields carved a path through them as if they weren't even there. The rearmost Kresh were the lowest forms, both Kresh and Kresh'Far. Kresh'Far in numbers can harm a Soulguard but Mageguards plowed through them.

I wanted to drop my shields and rip them apart with my bare hands and my monster was pounding at the walls of my mind. This wasn't the time for him. If I let him out, I wouldn't stop and reverse as I had directed. I had to keep him in check for now.

My inner struggle may have been the reason I missed the Ma'Nar that came up on our left. He was moving fast and he hit our flank.

I felt him as he slammed through our formation and ripped through the shield of one of our Mageguards. Simon Marko had never Pulled before but when the Kresh'Ma'Nar hit him, something in his chest cracked and his breath was gone. He latched onto the Ma'Nar and dragged himself against the beast and Pulled. Fire erupted from his body and the Ma'Nar ran back out of our formation roaring in pain.

There was a huge explosion to our right and we were thrown outward into the mass of Kresh.

"Reform!" I yelled, "Everyone else reverse course and get ready for the Alpha. We'll be there in a minute.

I should have been watching more closely when the Kresh'Ma'Nar had been inbound. Another Soul to add to those who had died for me. And the rage came out.

I Pulled and jumped, then lashed out with power at the horde of Kresh I had landed in. With glowing hands I ripped and tore them apart. An inhuman roar escaped my throat and I reveled in the death of my enemies.

The beast was out for only a minute, before I beat it back down and reformed my Juggernaut shield. I was covered in blood and I could feel the beast screaming inside me. I glanced back to see a path of body parts growing smaller as the horde closed in the hole I had left. My Squad had reformed as I had ordered and I returned to the spot I had vacated.

"Sorry," I said, "I got a little carried away."

"Ya think?" Prada asked.

"Let's join the others and give Simon a great big road paved with Kresh Souls for his trip home."

"Let's do it," Rostov said.

Our formation burst clear of the rear Kresh. We converged on the rest of our forces.

"Reyna," I said and she raised a shield.

"Code Alpha," I ordered, "Mageguards, link up Mages Pull on my mark."

I waited long enough for the links to my Mageguards to open up.

"Pull!"

I closed my eyes and used my Sight to target. I could see their Souls ahead of us and I could see their thoughts. Then Seventy Mages Pulled and I snatched that enormous reservoir of power. Fire gathered in the sky as the power grew and I began ripping gouts of fire down amongst them.

As I focused, the world slowed as it does when I fight with weapons. I saw the stronger Souls ahead of us and dropped gouts of fire on them.

RASH'TOR'RI!! Rang through their minds as four Kresh'Ma'Nar were incinerated by the dropping fire. I saw no more of them within range so I began dropping the gouts all over the horde that we had just gutted.

SCREAM FOR ME!!! My mental lash rolled through them.

I felt the fear in horde and it was contagious. It spread and they ran faster.

BUUURN!!

"Cease," I ordered and took what was left in the sky and slammed it down in a single blast that shook the ground.

There was silence.

"I hope there were enough of 'em for you to get home, Simon," I said softly.

I turned to find Dakarai looking at me. His soul showed fear, but it also showed much more. Perhaps Lyrica had been right. I always focused on the fear and never looked to see what else there was. There was satisfaction, there was hope, respect. If I just stopped with fear, I would have been wrong.

Just as I have probably been wrong for so many years. Sure, the fear is there and it hurts. But there is much more to people than that.

"I have heard of this Code Alpha," he said, "but to see it is truly beyond words."

"It's an experience," I said. "How many losses did we take?"

"Three," he said. "The Demon Mage hit two other formations before hitting yours. It killed two men before your man took it."

"I shoulda seen it," I said.

"You can't see everything, Rourke," he said. "None of us can. We just do our best and make our deaths honorable deaths."

"We bled them," Rostov said, "We lost three. They lost five Ma'Nar and thousands of soldiers and Kresh. Now we should go do it again and again. We will bleed them until they reach Cairo. Then we will show them what Hell looks like."

"You're right," I said, "so let's go do what we do best. Kill Kresh."

I saw nods from those who were close by.

"The juggernauts showed them one death," said Dakarai, "and the Alpha showed them another. Let us show them a death that we are all well suited for. We should do as you did. Let them see it up close and personal."

"Ok," I said, "but you'll have to call it, this time. When I let the beast out, I can't be the rational one."

"The Beast?"

"You saw a little of him back there," I said. "When I let it free it's hard to get the control back."

"He isn't lying," Prada said, "and those of us who're near him are the same."

"The Kresh DNA?"

I nodded. At least he knew about it and I wouldn't have to explain it again. Most of the higher ranks knew since my episode in Kansas where I tortured a Farrara'Ti's Soul after I ripped it from his body.

"Then I'll call it when we need to turn back and prepare for the Alpha," he said.

"Thank you," I said.

I hadn't done this since first Kansas. I had a hundred and ten men and women with me in my Squad. I would be projecting and we would move as a single entity. One seriously bloodthirsty entity.

We headed north to catch up with the horde of Kresh once more.

As we hit their rear, I let the beast out of its cage once more. Rage flooded my consciousness again and I was amongst them.

My emotions were projecting toward those with me and we all roared our fury. I let the beast run on autopilot and I watched with my Sight. This time, I saw the Kresh'Ma'Nar long before he reached us. He was surrounded by twenty Wraiths.

The second I saw them, everyone knew they were there through the link we shared. Ten Mages and a Soullord Pulled and discs exploded into the midst of the Wraiths, ripping them apart.

I continued forward, and before the Ma'Nar could launch its own fireballs at us, ripped its Soul from its body. Contact for that split second with their Source made me erupt with rage and hate. I had to stop doing that.

We continued our path of destruction through the center of the horde and I Lashed with my mind, as well.

I AM DEATH! DEVOURER OF SOULS!

My mental attacks served to add to the terror, I hoped. Otherwise I was just sounding corny quoting old sayings. Along with the fact I had just ripped the Soul from one of their "Cherished Ones", I think it was working.

"Reverse course, prepare for Code Alpha," Dakarai said through coms.

I began the struggle with the beast to push it back in the box I kept for it in my mind. It took a few moments to push it back down. It was harder than before. My dark side was getting stronger every time I touched their Source.

I managed to reestablish control and turned our group toward the rear again. There were more Kresh between us and the clearing but they scattered when they saw us coming. They had already gone through one of our passes and they didn't want anything to do with another.

Scattered or not, when we did the Code Alpha, hearing my telepathic lashes in their minds, they burned.

Chapter 33

Forty two times, we hit them over the day and a half it took to cross Ethiopia and the first half of Sudan. The Kresh had chosen the Nile River for their landmark, it seemed and they followed it north. After the fifteenth attack, we began seeing survivors behind the horde. They were feeling the pressure we were putting on their rear units.

"Sir," Dakarai said, "I understand the need for the psychological impact you have on the enemy. Have you considered the impact it may be having on our own men? What is that horrible noise?"

"That, my friend," I said, "is heavy metal."

I had taken out my mp3 player about four runs in and mounted it on my neck with a small shield. I put the earbud in on the side that I didn't wear coms. And I was projecting the music instead of threats by this time. It seemed to work as well as the telepathic taunts so I had continued. I didn't have to create a playlist, I love all of it.

"Drowning Pool, to be exact," I said, "What could be more appropriate than Bodies at a time like this?"

My group burst out the rear of the horde of Kresh we had just hit with juggernaut shields.

"But think of our men," he said. "The sheer emotional damage they must be suffering."

"That's funny, Ekene," I said. "Your daughter was singin' along a few minutes ago."

"Is this true, Adanna?"

"It might be," she said with a grin.

"A son," he said miserably, "It was all I asked for and I receive another crazy daughter."

She laughed and continued toward her spot in the formation.

"I can't believe he brought that stupid thing," Prada said. "At least the battery should die soon, and we'll have a little piece and quiet."

"Then you get to hear my jumbled versions as I try to remember all the words," I said.

"Good God!" Brighton yelled. "Does anyone have a charger? We can use one of the cars to charge it. Anyone? Please?"

"It's not that bad," I said.

"My ears bleed to even think about it," Adaya said.

"Hmmph, no appreciation for good music in the crowd."

"Pull!"

They Pulled and I grasped the power and thundered it down on the running Kresh. It just happened to accompany a scream from the song on the player. It was glorious. I may have giggled.

We can strive for peace as much as we want, but this is what I was made for. Despite the losses we had taken, the sheer death toll from all the civilians, all of it, I was having more fun than I had ever had.

And that's why I'm a monster. I feel the losses and they eat at me, but I was still having the time of my life as we killed them as fast as we could catch them.

Here we stood, covered in blood and dirt, looking at a plain littered with the twisted and burned bodies of the Kresh and I was grinning like a fool. What the Hell does that say about me?

"Was that a giggle?" Prada asked.

"I don't know what you're talkin' about."

"Hmmm."

"Sounded like a giggle to me," Adaya said.

My player shut down.

"Shit!" Adaya swore. Adaya never swore.

Adanna Dakarai stepped forward and handed me a charger for a car.

"Why would you bring a charger?" I asked.

"Why would you bring an mp3 player?" she asked with a shrug.

"Touche'," I said.

"Traitorous woman," her father mumbled. "A son would never have done this to me."

She laughed and returned to the formation.

***

"They don't retreat," Hicks said. "You can say that much for 'em."

"Yeah," Bill Tanner agreed, "but I'll never understand the bastards. After the losses they took when they hit the Israelis, how do they keep coming? It's like something is driving them. Those Farrara'Ti must have some serious mojo to keep them coming this strong."

Bill Tanner was a Soulguard who had been assigned to Hicks' squad, along with twenty others. They were to keep the snipers safe while they pick off Kresh. There were four snipers and four of what Hicks had discovered were called support Mages. They charged the ends of the barrels with their energy and the bullets would absorb that energy.

He'd seen Corn take out one of the big bastards a few hours earlier. The rest of his Marines had set up a perimeter along with the group of Guards.

"Corn," Hicks said, "Two o'clock."

"I see it," Corn answered and his rifle boomed.

"Good shot," Hicks said. "One less Wraith in there."

"Ooo-rah!"

"Wait a minute," Tanner said, "Did you see that?"

"Yeah, I did," Hicks said. "They all just turned west. What do ya think caused that? I know it wasn't Corn. He's a good shot but that was thousands that just looked like they panicked."

Corn's head popped up.

"What the Hell?" he asked. "Is that Five Finger Death Punch?"

They were all hearing it. Hicks could swear they were all hearing 'House of the Rising Sun' in their heads.

"Check your nine o'clock," Corn said, "'cause that looks like a group of ours. Jesus, those boys look rough.

"Holy Shit!" he continued. "It's that Rourke guy. Your girlfriend's with 'em."

"She's not my girlfriend," Hicks said.

"Never say no to a woman who can bench press a truck, Sir. Corn's rule, number one."

"I thought number one was just never say no to a woman."

"That was before I saw one that could bench press a truck."

"They all just headed west, Sir," Santos said. "Is it possible they were running from them."

He was pointing toward the group of incoming Soulguards.

"Hard to believe they were runnin' from a couple a hundred guys," Hicks said.

"I was at Second Kansas, Mister Hicks," Bill Tanner said, "and I guarantee they were running from him."

Hicks looked at him with a doubtful expression.

"Imagine what you saw in that valley you told me about. Then imagine it on a scale where the earth beneath the battlefield was turned to molten slag, and there were hundreds of thousands of Kresh burnt to ash."

Hicks nodded.

"They were running from him," Tanner said.

"Meanest son of a bitch on the planet," Hicks muttered to himself with a smile.

"What do you mean?"

"I told Rourke it's our job to be the meanest sons of bitches on the planet once."

"He is," Tanner said.

"For a mean son of a bitch, he's one Hell of a nice guy."

***

I saw their Souls on top of a building that looked like a steel plant or something. There were quite a few of them and one had just sniped a Wraith. I smiled as the imbued bullet hit the Wraith at the base of the skull.

"Prada," I said, "your boyfriend is on top of that building."

"Oh, no," she said.

"You'd think she'd be happy," Rostov said.

"Look at us, Alexei," Reyna said.

"We're covered in blood and dirt," Adaya said, "so what kind of impression would that make?"

"We're about to see," I said, "Hicks and a couple more are on their way down to meet us."

Hicks walked toward them with a Soulguard that I recognized. He was from California and was at Second Kansas.

"Hicks," I said, "and Tanner, isn't it?"

There was a fear in Tanner I was well familiar with. I see it in a lot of the ones who were at Second Kansas.

"Yes Sir," Tanner said.

"Looks like you been busy, Rourke," Hicks said. He was looking past me, and I could see what he was looking at in his mind.

Prada was hiding behind Samuel Drake, one of her Mageguards.

"Excuse me a minute, Rourke," Hicks said and walked straight toward Drake, who stepped aside.

Hicks walked up to Prada, and planted a kiss on her dirt and blood smeared lips.

"You said something about comparing scars," Hicks said, "and I'm holdin' ya to that."

He turned back around and grinned. Then he came back to the front of our group where I stood. Prada was like a deer in the headlights. Standing with her mouth hanging open.

"You seem to have taken my words to heart," he said, "They're runnin' from you?"

"Well, they're runnin' from us, actually," I said.

"I am going to say they are running from him," a seven foot tall black man said, "or more accurately, what he calls music. I have never been so happy to reach a war zone in my life."

"It wasn't so bad," one of the women behind him said.

"Silence! O' treacherous daughter."

She laughed.

"What's our situation up here?" I asked.

"They tried for the bridge across the canal," Hicks said, "but they hit the Israelis instead. Those Source Weapons ripped 'em up pretty bad."

"I had hopes for 'em," I said.

"The Egyptians came in from above the Israelis and hit 'em as well. Then the warships in the Red Sea opened up on 'em. We took huge losses because they wouldn't retreat, but they took worse."

I winced, "We may have had something to do with that."

"The Brits hit the scene about that time and the Chinese too. It was a Hell of a dust up. They were about to retreat and blow the bridge when the Kresh suddenly headed west into Cairo."

"Maybe we were a little too rough on 'em," I said. "We've been hittin' their rear from Ethiopia to the upper Sudan. There we took off east and headed up to join the forces up here. Where's our main base set up?"

"Our main command is in Israel but the local command is across the canal and north of the bridge. The Kresh don't swim, it seems."

"Their planet is mostly land mass," I said, "Kil'Sin'Deres told me they have about as much land as we have water and they aren't used to the restrictions it puts on 'em. That's why they stayed in Manhattan Island when they hit New York."

"That explains a lot."

"I think I should head to the local command and see what the whole situation is, and then we'll see where they want me to hit 'em."

"We'll accompany you," Hicks said. "It seems our area has a lack of targets."

Chapter 34

"You look terrible," Paige said when I walked into the building, "and you smell worse."

"No, really," I said, "tell me what you really think."

She laughed, "It's good to see you."

"How 'bout a hug?"

"I think not."

"So how's our situation?" I asked.

"They're in Cairo," she said, "though I don't know why, exactly. They were on the verge of breaking through when they just stopped and ran west. Did you have anything to do with that?"

"Maybe," I said. "I heard they wouldn't retreat. They took huge losses but wouldn't retreat. I'm afraid I may have been part of the reason. We've been hitting the rear for days, and I've been Lashing them with the telepathy. We were hoping we could drive 'em fast enough that they wouldn't have time to kill everyone in the towns along the way."

"It worked," I said, "because we found a lot of survivors and sent 'em west. Unfortunately it cost a lot of soldiers' lives here. Maybe if we hadn't driven 'em so hard..."

"When we have a choice of soldiers or civilians, we have to choose civilians, Colin," Gregor said.

"Do we have enough forces to assault Cairo?" I asked.

"No way," Gregor said. "We were about to have to fall back across the channel and blow the bridge."

"Then we need to drop a Code Alpha on 'em in Cairo."

"We've been informed that 'under no circumstances are we to destroy Cairo as we did in New York.'"

"It wouldn't be anything like New York," I said, "probably level the whole city."

"Therefore, not an option."

"Do the Egyptians have the forces to remove several million Kresh from Cairo?" I asked.

"No they don't," Paige said.

"What, exactly, do they want?" I asked.

"What they really want is the Kresh gone with no damage to their city. That's probably not going to happen."

"Yeah, that's not gonna happen."

"Have you got any ideas?" she asked.

"I've got one," I said. "I go kill a Farrar'Ti, and lure the Kresh out of Cairo."

"And how the Hell are you going to do that?" she asked.

"In short," I said, "I say we drop in from above as soon as I locate the Farrara'Ti. I kill it. We run like Hell."

"Colin," Gregor said, "this isn't a thousand Kresh, not even a hundred thousand Kresh. There are millions."

"I know," I said, "and I would rather drop an Alpha on their heads. But we have to try to do as they ask. If it fails, we drop the Alpha wherever we have to. It would be easier to sneak in alone but if I have to Alpha, I need the troops. I'll take twenty Mages."

"No, you'll take a full load," Paige said. "You can fit a hundred and ten on the plane. Take a hundred and ten. Don't even argue with me on this, because there are over four million Kresh in there."

"Then that's what I'll do," I said. "Now I'm goin' to clean some of this shit off me and go see Lyr. Then I'll gather the troops."

This whole thing grated at me. Buildings can be replaced as long as the people survive. Everything depended on whether the damn things would chase me anyway. I'd chased them for two and a half days. Would they be angry enough to chase me after I killed their Farrara'Ti?

Maybe. If not, then I would blow up Cairo.

I left the office that Paige and Gregor had been using for the last few days, whenever they weren't out on the lines with the other Mages.

If not for the Source weapons, the lines would have collapsed. There weren't enough Mages to have stopped what the Kresh threw at them.

Prada was outside waiting.

"How bad is it?" she asked.

"Looks like we get to jump out of a plane again," I said.

She sighed.

"We got our mission," I said, "so get cleaned up, go jump Hicks' bones, then meet back here in three hours. We're about to start a ruckus."

"Oh, goody," she said, "I was gettin' bored."

"Tell the others as you go," I said. "I gotta go tell Lyr I need her to stay behind, again."

"Good luck with that," she said.

I nodded and headed toward the tents to the north. All the wounded were being evacuated to Jerusalem but I knew Lyr would be there, healing any she could as they waited for their rides.

"Boss!" I heard from my left.

I turned to find Trent, "We got a temporary barracks over here to get cleaned up and re-armored."

"Not much point," I said, "but I can use a few hours of clean before we head back out."

"Where we goin'?"

"You're with Lyr," I said, "because I'm takin Mages only on this one. We're gonna kill a Farrara'Ti and kick the hornets' nest."

"She's gonna be pissed if ya leave her behind again."

"I know, but I need someone to save our asses if this all goes to Hell."

"Hmmm."

I followed Trent inside where I found the most wonderful thing, a shower and a whole new set of combat armor.

After the refreshing shower and some clean clothes, I continued my trek to the tents of injured. I felt her Pulling before I reached the tents. She was bent over a man and holding his leg.

I could see the flow of life force as it focused right on the spot where his leg had been broken.

As she finished, I stepped into the tent and she saw me. A huge smile crossed her face and she was in my arms.

"I've got good news and bad news," I said. "Good news is that we're back, the bad news is we have to go back out again."

"When do we go?"

"Here's the thing..."

"Don't say it if it's a lie." She said.

"I really may need you to come save our asses," I said.

"That wasn't even a lie," she said, "What the Hell are you about to go do?"

"Gonna kick a hornets' nest and see if we can lure 'em outta Cairo for an Alpha."

"If we could only do an Alpha in Cairo," she said.

"You saw 'em too?" I asked.

"Yes, and I was still tempted to do the Alpha."

"I was too."

I told her of the Egyptians' demands. I would have ignored them if it wasn't for the Souls I saw as I looked toward Cairo. They had a group of prisoners on the northwest end of the city. Perhaps ten thousand souls.

"We have to try to pull 'em out away from those people," I said. "If it doesn't work, it doesn't work but we gotta try."

"What do you need me to do?"

"Gather all the Mages and Mageguards. Have 'em ready for an Alpha. When we reach a certain point, be ready to initiate it."

"Ok," she said, "but I still wish we could just hit it from outside and let them rebuild."

"I do, too," I said. "We'll try to save their city if we can, but as soon as we get far enough away from those people, do it. Meanwhile, is there anything I can do to help you here?"

"There's a lot of wounded," she said. "Start anywhere. If it's too severe, holler and I'll make sure we can do it."

"Will do," I said.

***

"Where's he at?" Gregor asked Paige.

"Down in the tents," she answered, "helping Lyrica heal the wounded."

"Not so much of a monster as he thinks," he said.

"He never was as much of a monster as he thinks he is," she said, "and never will be."

"We should tell the Egyptians to piss up a rope and burn the whole place down," Kharl said from behind them.

"I know we should," Gregor said, "But Colin has a point. We have to at least try to meet their demands. It is their country."

"He's tryin' to do the 'right' thing," Kharl said.

"He always tries," Paige said, "and I guess I'll show him my support. I'll be going with him."

"As will I," Gregor said.

"Can we afford to have all three of you out there in that at once?" Kharl asked.

"He needs the strongest Mages with him and we are the strongest Mages," Paige said.

"Just as well," Kharl said, "I'm goin' with about half the Jaeghernauts. I've been through the classes, I just prefer usin' the Mageguard skills. Doesn't mean I can't Pull, if necessary."

Chapter 35

The plane ride would be short but necessary. I needed to get high up and look down to see if I could find the Soul of the Farrara'Ti.

"Do you see it?" Paige asked.

"Yeah," I said, "it's in the northwest."

It was near the prisoners. I hadn't told anyone about the prisoners. If this didn't work, I didn't want my people carrying the guilt with them about the loss. If we couldn't get the Kresh far enough away from the prisoners to hit them, that would be on me. Not them.

I pulled the street map of Cairo out and lay it on the floor.

"This building," I said as I pointed at a large structure a short distance from the Nile, "this is our target. We jump and use shield chutes. Quiet landing. I'll go down inside the building and kill the Farrara'Ti. When all hell breaks loose I'm coming out on the south east end and we meet there.

"Then we juggernaut shield up and head south east as fast as we can."

"Sounds like a plan," Prada said. "What are we gonna do if something goes wrong?"

"Same as we always do."

"Make some shit up," Rostov said.

"Oh, dear," Paige said with a sad shake of her head, "and this is what you call normal?"

"The life of a Soullord's Guard is an exciting life, Ma'am," Brighton said, "and just full of adventure, full of surprises."

"Full of shit," Kharl said.

"That, too, Mate," Brighton said with a grin.

"I'm so glad you made it in time for this, Daphne," Kharl said. "We were hopin' ya might lose yer cloths again. You wearin' a thong?"

"Bite me," Daphne Cavanaugh said, "and dream on. You keep runnin' your mouth and I'll tell Ky. I hear she has a stream bigger than yours and can throw you through walls."

"Speakin of that," he said, "Ya really screwed me on that one, Son. I thought ya had my back."

"It was the only way she'd do it," I said. "She said I couldn't stop till she was stronger than you."

"Traitor," he said.

"Comin' up on our drop point, Sir," the pilot's voice came over coms.

"Roger," I said and the back door began to lower.

"Everybody ready?" I asked.

"Ready as I'll eve..."

I threw Prada out of the plane.

"Did you just...?" Paige started.

"Yep," I said, "you need help?"

"No, thank you," she said and jumped with Gregor right behind her.

Rostov went by laughing. It never gets old, throwing Prada out of a plane.

I jumped and dove down to the same level as Paige. She hadn't done many chute drops and I thought I might need to help. She handled it like a professional and looked at me with one eyebrow raised as I flew past. I opened the portal on my chute and my plummet turned into a slow glide.

This was probably the slowest I had jumped out of one of the planes, but we were on a secret mission. It wouldn't do to land in an explosion of fire and death, now, would it?

As I got nearer to the ground, I looked around at the city sprawled below us. Buildings upon buildings stretched in every direction. Cairo was huge. And the streets were packed with Kresh.

"We'll have to go south on top of the buildings," I said over coms. "There's too many of 'em in the streets."

"Roger," Paige said.

"Be ready when I kill the Farrara'Ti," I said. "Don't wait for me, but I'll be right behind you."

I landed on the roof of our target along with a hundred and nine Mages.

"You know what happens when we kill one of 'em. I'll be movin' fast as I come back out of the building. You guys need to be moving already. And we'll need to make a lot of noise, so feel free to blast the shit out of 'em."

They started moving quietly to the south end of the building.

Rostov motioned for Daphne to precede him, "Perhaps you may lose your clothes again, and I would not wish to miss this."

"Never goin' on a date again," she muttered as she went by him.

"Do not say such things," Rostov said. "Perhaps you should have been with a Russian who would have gladly removed his clothing and fought, naked, beside such a woman. It would have been glorious!"

"Crazy bloody Russian," Stone said as he walked by me.

"Russians are all crazy, Lad," Lennox Flynn said, "Tis a proven fact, that."

I chuckled as my friends headed to the south. With a little searching, I found the access to the building. I focused on a thought of empty space and projected it. This was a trick Gorvelis had told me about while I was on Cerres. The key is to keep your mind clear. Which is much harder than you may think.

I opened the door and began a quiet descent down to the bottom floor of either an apartment building or a hotel. I could feel the presence of the Farrara'Ti below me.

My rage was trying to beat down the walls but this was no place for that. Slowly I descended until I was at the last floor. I eased through the door into a lobby. He was waiting for me.

Rash'Tor'Ri, he said into my mind, **I feel you.**

Not for long, I thought back at him.

He was moving. Like Kil'Sin'Deres, he moved like lightning. I dodged to the side but not fast enough. Pain exploded in my right side as his claws ripped my side open.

His body slammed into the wall behind me, because his Soul was gripped in my right hand. I felt their Source and the beast inside me howled.

Blood flowed down my left side but everything seemed to move right so I Pulled power to the spot and the blood flow slowed.

A roar filled the air throughout the city as the Kresh realized what had happened.

"Damn," I muttered, "gotta move."

My side wasn't healed but there were crashes as the Kresh slammed into the side of the building in their rush to get to me.

I ran up the stairs with crunches, crashes, and roars following behind me.

"They sound pissed," Kharl said over coms.

"They are," I grunted as my side ached, "and I'm on my way back up."

I reached the roof to find some of the Mages waiting on me, Kharl and my ten squad leaders.

"Paige took the rest ahead and started raising Hell," Kharl said. "We're your escort."

"By all means," I said, "let's get the Hell outta here then."

We ran south as the top of the building erupted in Kresh.

"Son of a bitch!" Prada said, "that's a lot of Kresh."

"Tis a fact," Flynn said.

I kept Pulling to the wound in my side and, after a few minutes, stopped lagging behind.

"You're hurt," Kharl said. "Why didn't ya say somethin'?"

"That bastard was fast," I said, "and I've got it healed mostly."

As we leaped to the next building, we all launched discs down into the horde.

They launched fireballs back that missed us.

"Demon Mages," I said.

"Really? Ya think?" Prada asked.

"Smart ass."

She laughed.

I felt a large Pull from ahead of us.

"Paige or Gregor," I said, "they got a shitload of Kresh following 'em."

I could see the dark Souls ahead of us where our other group were located. We were almost caught up when I saw them go to the ground. There was a huge train yard ahead and we had to cross it.

"Get ready for juggernauts," I said.

As we left the edge of the last building, we spread out and opened portals on the juggernaut armor. I slammed into the packed Kresh in front of me and blood arced upwards. We broke through to the open space where Paige and the rest were running across the train yard.

Then I saw past them.

"Oh shit," I said as Kresh poured into the yard from all directions.

They were moving at full speed and hit our juggernauts with a huge crunch. A Mage with juggernaut shields can do a god awful amount of damage, but it requires being able to move. There were so many Kresh we actually ground to a halt and they kept coming.

Chapter 36

I'd never seen anything like this. They piled higher and higher. In moments, only the strongest of us were even still moving.

"We have to close ranks," I said on coms.

I saw Adaya's shield collapse. She was about forty feet to my right and I could hear the thoughts in her mind as the dead Kresh fell in on top of her.

Don't do it, Adaya, I am coming! I said into her mind as she was screaming.

I Pulled and dropped my shield in the right side. My Soullance fired and I burned a hole in the dead Kresh. I followed at Mage speed so the bodies couldn't collapse in the hole I bored.

Then I felt her hands grab my leg and blew a hole around us and slammed a shield out. I was Pulling and reinforcing the shield.

We have to move to the others, I said into her mind as she was calming her panic.

"Follow, close, Adaya," I said on coms.

Kharl was the next one to the right, but his shield was holding. Lennox was the furthest away but his shield suddenly went super bright.

Flynn!

I heard him in his mind and felt the burning pain, "Get 'dem out, me boy."

The ground shook as he Pulled too much. His last action was to Pull everything he could and a huge hole was blasted in the bodies.

It freed the rest of our party and we closed the distance before the Kresh could fill the gap. I slammed a shield out and reinforced it with a Pull. I was probably the only one who could do that for any length of time. That's what had gotten Flynn.

His shields weren't strong enough to hold and he'd been Pulling to keep them strong enough.

"Paige is about a hundred feet that way," I said, pointing, "As I clear a path, we need to move together."

"Do it, Son," Kharl said.

"Goodbye, my friend," I muttered and looked back to where Flynn had been.

I opened the end toward where I could see the others. I Pulled and the Soullance spit fire again. We closed the distance and I opened a hole in her shield that we all squeezed through.

She was Pulling to support the shield and I could see the power in her was past dangerous. I ran to her and touched her shoulder. The excess power in her was enormous but I took it and launched it upwards through a hole I opened in her shield.

I stopped when it was safe for her to continue.

"I'm pretty sure," she said, "we're still in Cairo."

"Lovely city," I said, "Thinkin' about buying a vacation home here."

"Just so you all know," I said, "if we don't make it out of this, we didn't do this for real estate. There were about ten thousand prisoners in the northwest corner of the city."

"That sounds ominous," Kharl said. "Isn't this the part where you make some shit up?"

I felt a massive Pull and looked up.

"Holy shit!" I said, "Shields! Now! Everyone!"

"What the Hell?!" Prada exclaimed.

We all felt the Pull that was happening to our east.

"The Alpha and the Omega, the beginning and the end," I muttered.

"You quotin' the bible now?" Kharl asked as he slammed his shield against the inside of Paige's.

Everyone was looking at me as if I was crazy. I was laughing as the whole world began to shake around us.

***

"Advance all troops toward Cairo," Dietrich said, "that's the advice I would give."

"You're in charge, Dietrich," Lyrica said, "I'm just the weapon. You know what I need. Make it happen."

"Yes Ma'am," he said and started spouting the orders to move the troops toward Cairo.

Lyrica watched the plane circling above Cairo. Time to move, she thought.

She headed down from the building she was perched atop. The Mages and Mageguards were ready and the regular troops had already moved out.

"Let's go," she said.

She jogged toward Cairo and they followed. I wish we could've just dropped the sky on them, she thought. She had a bad feeling about this.

They reached a factory, outside of Cairo. She climbed the wall with the rest right behind her.

Then she felt the Pulls. Her sight opened and she looked, intently toward the city. She watched two groups of Souls running south. But she also saw all of those dark Souls closing from all directions.

"Dear God," she said, "supports, link up!"

"How many, Ma'am?"

"Everyone!"

"Prepare for Omega."

She turned to find one of the Egyptians.

"We will not participate in an attack within our city..."

"You'll do what needs to be done or my company will pull the contracts with your government. You'll not receive another weapon nor a replacement piece for the ones you have. Your contract states that in a situation where Omega is deemed necessary, your troops will participate. You break your contract and you're on your own."

"But..."

He looked into her eyes as the fire began to flow across her body.

"They will be ready," he said.

She turned back to see piles of Kresh higher than buildings.

"Omega! I repeat, Omega!"

The world erupted in fire.

Omega hadn't been tried by either her or Colin as of yet. It was a theoretical action to use when there wasn't enough power in an Alpha.

An Alpha used the power of the Mages around the Soullord. The strongest Alpha either had used was several hundred Mages.

What launched into the night sky was the fire from thirty two thousand Source weapons.

The streams of four hundred Mages and six hundred Mageguards thrummed as Lyrica reached to the sky and seized that power.

She moved it to a point above the Kresh that covered the bright Souls below. Then she dropped that massive maelstrom down on top of the gigantic pile of Kresh.

***

I laughed. The world shook. The Kresh burned. Everyone looked at me like I was insane. It was, swiftly, becoming a beautiful day.

When the power hit our shields, everyone staggered with the force of that Maelstrom.

I laughed harder and pulled the excess power from any of them who had built up too much. Then I added it to the shield.

Then it was over and the power dispersed.

We looked up into the night sky and lowered our shields. The air stank of burnt flesh and blood, but it was air. Under the pile, we had been swiftly running out of air.

The Source can keep you going without food. It can sustain you without water, but even the Source can't replace air.

Lennox Flynn had saved us all when he Mage bombed. The time it would have taken to free all of the squad would have had us outside of Paige's shield. Paige would have overloaded and that's something no one wants to see. The man had literally saved us all.

We climbed over the charred remains of so many Kresh, but there was really no describing it. The others had quit their mad dash to kill us and scattered in all directions. The Souls I could see were filled with terror.

Adaya looked back down into that hole where we had been and her whole body shook. She had been close to doing what Lennox had done.

When we all come out of that darkness there were twenty one of our dead left behind.

"I should have told them about the prisoners," I said. "They shouldn't have died thinkin' it was about real estate."

"Why didn't you?" Paige asked.

"If we had needed to Alpha right on top of it," I said, "I didn't want that to be on the conscience of anyone but me."

"That's a lot to take on yourself, Son," Kharl said.

"At least we pulled 'em far enough out, they didn't get hit," I said, looking north. I had been afraid to look that direction but I finally worked up the nerve. The bright Souls of humans still shone where they had been.

"What say we go set 'em free?" I said.

"Let's do that," Adaya said.

We set off toward the warehouses the Kresh had used to hold the prisoners.

Chapter 37

We walked out of Cairo with three quarters of the Mages that had gone in with us. We also walked out with eleven thousand four hundred and eighty two freed Egyptians.

I saw Lyrica's Soul flood with sorrow as she saw who was missing from our ranks. She had become friends with Lennox while she spent two years in Scotland.

She met me with an embrace.

"I'm sorry," I whispered.

"Me too," she whispered, "but for now we put on a brave face and save the crying for later."

"Agreed," I said.

We turned and walked toward the Allied base beside the canal.

"They scattered in every direction after that," Lyrica said. "They thought it was Rash'Tor'Ri that had done it to them."

"It was," I said. "We are Rash'Tor'Ri. They don't quite understand that yet."

I looked back toward Cairo with a fire burning in my Soul that just would not stop.

"They will," she said with that same fire burning inside her Soul.

***

"We need to set up patrols to go out and hunt 'em down," I said.

"I think Ekene Dakarai should head up that operation," Paige said from behind me, "because it is his territory. We'll give any support he needs."

We stood in an office looking at the map on the wall. There were pins in it marking forces that were moving through Cairo and the surrounding area.

"That sounds like a plan," I said. "Dakarai is a good choice. Besides, you two are gonna be busy with the politics. We just blew up a large chunk of Cairo."

"This war took a toll on the whole Delta," Gregor said, "and it will take some time for Egypt to recover. They fared much better than Kenya. They had time to evacuate the majority of their people from the area, Kenya had no warning and not enough forces to hold them. Ethiopia and Sudan fared better because they were moving much faster for some reason."

"Yes, I wonder what that was," Paige said.

"I have no idea what you are talking about," I said.

Gregor chuckled, "I'll see you two later. I have to go see some of those politicians right now."

"I'd rather be on patrol," I said.

"Wouldn't we all," he said.

"I have to go, too," Paige said. "I'll send Dakarai to you, Colin."

"Thanks," I said, "and I've got a lot of paperwork to do now. I'd rather be on patrol than this, too."

"True," she said.

As they left the room, I walked to the desk to confront one of the hardest tasks I had ever done. The list of casualties was much larger than any I had had before.

Estimated, nearly fifty million civilian deaths in Africa and Europe. The number was hard to wrap my head around. I had expected a large death toll when the Kresh came back but these numbers were hard to take.

Do I have the right to decide not to close the gates permanently? Where do I draw the line? There are billions of humans on the other worlds and they are enslaved by the Kresh. I must let millions die to save the billions. I understand the logic, but I have a difficult time being that calculating.

The toll in civilians was horrible and the toll in soldiers was staggering. It seems that we missed one hell of a battle while we were chasing Kresh through Africa. The sheer numbers of the dead sent a chill down my spine.

It was estimated thirty eight thousand Soulguards died at the Battle of the Delta. Soldiers from the various countries numbered close to two million and the deaths were over thirty percent.

Warships in both the Red Sea and the Gulf of Suez had been firing non-stop into the Kresh. Bombers from all over the world had been dropping ordinance on them. And still they took out a third of the forces facing them and had nearly four million Kresh in Cairo when we killed the Farrara'Ti.

I knew a lot of Soulguards and I knew I would be seeing a lot of familiar names in the lists I was staring at.

My run through Africa had begun with seventy three Mages and three hundred and ninety Mageguards. I had lost ninety eight Mageguards and twelve Mages. Then I lost another twenty one Mages in Cairo. These were my personal losses.

I knew the next few days were going to be rough. I was about to write each one of their next of kin. A generic letter wouldn't do. I must remember all of them. I must always remember those that gave their lives for me. Never become uncaring of those losses. When I don't care anymore, that is when the Monster has truly taken over.

I started with Jimmy Sandoval. He had been in Tennessee when I was posted there as Mage Captain. He was a card player and had been obsessed with an old song from Kenny Rogers, The Gambler.

I wrote the letter to his son, James Sandoval II. He was a grandfather, himself, and he had known of the Soulguard for his entire life.

Hour after hour, I wrote to children, grandchildren, brothers, and sisters. There were many who had no families and I marked them as well. I will remember, even if no one else will.

I came down to Lennox Flynn. He had a daughter who was a Mage in Argentina. I wrote her of her father's heroic sacrifice.

As he had exploded, he had raised a shield up around him that reached about four feet. It kept the blast from killing those around him, yet still destroyed enough Kresh to break them all free.

He was a good man, and I had known him from the day he presided over my trial when Gavin Price had tried to tie me from the Source and failed. Price had died and the Council had tried to charge me.

Flynn had seen through the bullshit and had been a supporter of me and mine ever since.

He had just gotten back from London in time to follow me to his death.

There was a knock on my door. I looked up to see Dakarai's Soul through the door.

"Come in, Ekene," I said.

"I understand you wish to see me," he said.

"We have a mission for ya," I said. "We need you to set up the patrols to hunt down the rest of 'em."

"It will be done," he said.

"Good," I said, "And we'll support anything ya need. Planes, guns, Guards, whatever ya need. Let me know."

He nodded.

"I also have a few questions," I said. "Have a seat. I have some names here from our losses on our way up through Africa. I'd like to know a little bit about 'em."

"Why?" he asked, but he already knew why.

"I need to know these men because they died under my command. I need to remember 'em all so I don't forget the price we have to pay. I need to..."

"I understand," he said with a reassuring smile, "and it means a great deal to know you are that sort of commander. Some look at losses as numbers. It is much easier to spend numbers than names. Which names do you wish to know about? Shall we start with Ebele Jabari?"

I nodded.

"She was born in Kenya seventy three years ago and her name means compassion and courage. She was blessed with ample quantities of both. She had family in Nairobi."

I listened to Dakarai as he talked through a list of men and women who had been killed in action through our trek.

He knew their names and he knew them all. I knew Dakarai was the one who needed to head up the operation in Africa, beyond the shadow of a doubt, after we talked for three hours.

Chapter 38

I walked around the corner to find Prada in the arms of Sergeant Hicks.

"Be careful," she said, "I don't want anything to happen to that pretty face."

"Don't worry 'bout me, girl," he said. "I'm too damn mean to die."

He had a Source weapon and the helmet laying on a pack behind them.

She kissed him and was gone in an instant. He turned to find me standing there.

"Damn woman's fast," he said, "tough as nails, too. She'd make a good Marine."

"She's one of the best," I said. "You could do a lot worse."

"I'm in total agreement with ya on that, Sir."

"You guys headin' out to hunt?"

"Yep," he said, "got me one of these new guns of yours. Itchin' ta try it out on some Kresh. Corn has a tagalong Mage to keep his bullets charged, and half my platoon has the new guns."

"Sounds dangerous," I said. "Marines with Source weapons."

"Ooo-rah!"

I laughed, "Seriously, you guys be careful out there. You need support, call us."

"Damn right," he said, "Then you can drop the right hand of God on 'em. Or just drop your girlfriend on 'em. I'm a damn Marine and that woman scares me. She's healin' folks, and all of a sudden, she's a nuclear bomb. Then she's right back to healin' folks."

"Thank God she's on our side," I said.

"No doubt," he said, "just don't piss her off, I kinda like ya."

"I try my best not to," I said.

"Be sure you don't," he said, "we need you two. This was going south pretty bad before you got up here."

"These had a healthy fear of me after my little trip over to their world. If it wasn't for that, we'd probably have been rolled right over at the Gate."

"What'd ya do over there?"

"Me and one of *them* killed two of the Farrara'Ti that were next to come here."

"One of them?"

"Yeah," I said. "It was hard for me to accept, at first. Some of 'em are different. We have a whole other kind of war goin' on over there. My people are building their forces to take Hub, the city that has all the Gates to the other worlds. It takes time. If we can hold out long enough, the war here will end from that side."

He nodded, "More goin' on than they let a Sergeant know about."

"There's a lot goin' on alright," I said, "and we need it to happen as quickly as possible. This clan was a small clan with a strong fear already in place. There're clans over there that make these look like children kickin' ant hills."

"We need to mop these up as quickly as we can then," he said, "and get ready for another wave."

"That's right, but don't get in too big of a hurry and get careless," I said. "We need everyone we can get to be ready for the next one."

"Have we got any ideas where the next one may be?"

"None," I said, "but I don't think they'll try Kansas again. They won't be able to come here again if our dam worked. Which is something I have to look into soon. And they can't use the Gate in Romania. It leaves four other positions, if my intel is right."

"How sure are you that there are only seven Gates?"

"Pretty sure," I said. "Kil'Sin'Deres was the Kresh in charge of our world for a long time and he confirmed it. He didn't use the big Gates so he didn't know their exact locations, though."

"He was the one who was killin' humans all those years and now he's an ally?"

There was a little coldness in his words.

"I understand how you feel, Hicks," I said. "He was the one behind my parent's deaths. If I can get past that, I think most folks should be able to get past his history."

"He's the reason we can face this with a gun in hand," I said. "He let us get far enough advanced to be a foe that would unite his people. It didn't work so he came to me and pledged his people to me. Now he's using my name to unite his people another way."

"And if he turns on you?"

"He can't now," I said. "The one thing that's been a weakness in the Kresh is also one of their greatest strengths. They're telepathic. They communicate during battle that way."

"What's that got to do with him turnin' on you?"

"The more powerful of the telepaths use that mental strength to place their Mark on those they control. I inherited this power when I was born with their DNA in my blood. I Marked Kil'Sin'Deres and he won't turn on me."

"Sounds complicated and dangerous," he said, "but that begs the question of why didn't you use it on the Kresh here?"

"When I use the Mark, it works on both Kresh and Human because I am a bridge between both. There are seventy four Romanians who live in Oklahoma on a farm I bought for 'em. I Marked 'em when I didn't know what I was doin'. I'm fighting to free Humanity, I won't enslave it to save it."

"What if it's the only way to survive this?"

"When we were under that pile of Kresh out there," I said, "I could have Lashed with the Mark. If I did, I would have Marked eighty nine of my brothers and sisters."

"They would live," he said.

I could tell he was playing Devil's Advocate. I could see his approval of my choice in his Soul.

"Live free or die," I said, "it's not just a quote. I took those Romanians' freedom from them and I will pay for that the rest of my life. I won't take another Human's freedom."

"You're a good man, Rourke," he said, "Many a man would use that to take power."

"The Kresh won't accept any other way than the Mark," I said, "and Kil'Sin'Deres is spreading my Mark across his world. I'm not as good as you may think. I'm enslaving a race that was originally created to be slaves. They broke free and I am placing them right back where they began."

"Perhaps it's a new destination instead of back to the beginning," he said. "What does this Mark do?"

"It places an imprint of everything that makes me who I am into their mind. They make decisions based on that imprint. They'll follow any order I give 'em. I think that's what it means to be a slave. And I'm enslaving a world."

"I guess the harsh reality of it is this," Hicks said. "If you weren't, could we survive a war with their whole race? And, if so, could you leave that other world of Humans being enslaved and murdered to their fates? It would be a hard decision, but I feel like you've already chosen. You can't desert another whole world of Humans."

"Fourteen worlds," I said. "But if it had been even a single world, I'd still choose the path I'm walkin'. I can't choose any other. I swore to protect Humanity from the dark, and I can't limit that to just a small piece of Humanity."

"I'm glad I'm just a lowly Sergeant," Hicks said.

"Sometimes, I wish I could be too."

"Time to hit the road, Rourke," he said. "Be careful and try to keep Andrea straight."

"That's a full time job, all by itself."

He laughed and picked up his pack.

As he walked away I said, "Good luck."

"Don't need luck," he said, "I got a platoon of Marines."

I love Marines.

Chapter 39

"It looks alright but if you want it to stay for good, you need some spillways up there and some bracing in the middle," Jack said, "See the bulging inward of the interior shield?"

We were looking at the shield dam Lyrica and I had built to flood the gate. It was holding back about twenty feet of water at the moment.

"Yeah," I said, "I see it."

"If you brace laterally, you'll give it enough strength to hold the weight. You need the spillways so the water will drain off in the right place. If not, it's gonna flood the whole width of the dam and weaken the ground."

"Then the whole thing falls," I said.

"Exactly."

I was keeping the shields lit up so he could examine them. I stopped and my Soulstream stopped flowing power into me.

The manipulation of shields had become second nature to me and I used my mind to pull two channels down lower over the river bed. Now the water would spill out there when it reached about thirty five feet. Then I began crafting a shield from my stream. It Ran between the two sides of our dam to support the weight as Jack had said.

When it was done, I lit it up again.

"That should do it, Sir," Jack said, "though not necessarily an engineered dam but it'll hold."

I formed a tendril at either end of my construct and pushed the far end into the Source. The power flowed toward me and at the last second I pushed the other into the Source and cut my tie.

It Thrummed with power and became solid.

"That has to be the best thing in the world," Jack said, "to be able to see that all the time."

"It's given me a hell of an advantage," I said. "If I had half the education you have, I'd be dangerous."

"From what I hear, it would just interfere with a lot of the things you do," he said. "The education would tell you some of the things you've done are impossible. Then you wouldn't have tried it. It would be handy at times like these, but I think you do just fine without it."

"I suppose," I said.

"Plus we wouldn't have gotten to see the video they play at the academy of a youngster getting blown across the Dome."

"They still play that?"

"For every new class, and anytime someone comes through that hasn't seen it."

I sighed.

The Soul Grenades had been discovered in that incident and proven quite useful at times. I was much more careful after that. Who am I kidding? I blew myself up pretty regular for about five years.

"These days, I blow other stuff up," I said, "instead of blowin' myself up."

"Yeah," he said, "they show those videos too."

"I almost wish they wouldn't," I said, "but everyone needs to know what may be happenin' at any moment."

"True," he said.

"Have ya given any thought to my offer?" I asked.

"Yeah," he said. "I find the whole thing fascinating and I'll gladly consult with your guys in Tennessee."

"Good, we could use your talents. I need bigger versions of the weapons. Somethin' we can use on a larger scale."

"I have some ideas, Sir," he said.

"Good," I said, "and I need someone who can build these things without my advantage. Things would have gone quite different if Lyrica had been somewhere else last week. I need people who can carry on without me if something like that happens again."

"I see," he said. "I'll do my best."

"I know you will, Jack," I said, "I saw that in your Soul the first day I met you."

***

An Awards ceremony was held at the Academy in Scotland. We had been cleaning up the wreckage in the Delta for a month and getting accurate counts on the men and women we lost.

It was a hard thing to see when we looked at the numbers. I couldn't help but put faces with the numbers and it made for a difficult day.

"I wished to award this Medal of Valor, personally," I said to the crowd in front of me, "Because this medal belongs to a man who saved my life as he gave his. Lennox Flynn was my friend. He will be sorely missed. I would like to present this medal to Glynnis Flynn, Len's daughter."

I handed the small box to the petite red haired woman who came forward.

"He was a good man," I said softly to her, "and I'm sorry I couldn't stop what happened."

"Ye ha' no idea how proud 'e was ta be chosen ta be in ye personal guard, Sir," she said in a familiar Scottish accent. I could hear him in every word she said.

"It was my honor," I said with a lump in my throat.

She nodded and returned to her seat.

I also sat down. I don't know how Paige had stood up there and done the whole ceremony. That was the only award I actually gave out, personally and I had almost caved.

The ceremony continued and our dead were honored. Those that had been victorious were recognized and the world turned on. We still hunted for Kresh in Africa, they were quiet and hiding in the jungles of central Africa.

New patches were given to all that were present at the battles. The Battle of the Delta, Assault on Cairo, African Run, Kenya Gateway,

Istanbul, Vienna, Prague, London, Berlin, and a single patch given out for Paris, France. One Mage in the right place at the right time.

There had been skirmishes up and down the Nile River as people had been evacuating. All of these were honored, as well.

It was still something relatively new to the Soulguard to do all of the recognition.

I didn't want any awards but they made me take the Distinguished Service Medal anyway. I hate to be recognized for just doing my job, but so many feel the same way and still accept theirs, so who am I to refuse?

All in all, it was a very difficult day.

The evening was much better. Lyrica and I had dinner in London. I had never been to London except as a fly through. It was different, but it still felt familiar as we sat and ate dinner. People really aren't so different from one place to the next.

Epilogue

The Prophet stood on a roof top in Hub. He was waiting for a meeting. Bel and her Squad stayed back, in case this went wrong. It was hard for them to place their trust in one of the Masters. They would lie to a Human without a qualm.

A huge Kresh walked out of the darkness.

"He's alone," Bel said, "so at least he kept his word."

"He's a Farrara'Ti," Vita said. "He can take care of himself. Watch closely, we may only have a fraction of a moment to act."

"Worry not," the Farrara'Ti spoke, "Rash'Tor'Ri would be quite upset if I attacked his best friend."

"I saw you once," the Prophet said, "in Montana."

"Yes," Kil'Sin'Deres said.

"You're the one he sent those Kresh he Marked to."

"I carry his Mark, as well, Rictor Hughes," he said, "My name is Kil'Sin'Deres and I am your ally."

"And what is it you would ask of me, Kil'Sin'Deres?" Rictor asked.

"Without the Mark," he said, "I know you will have difficulty trusting me. Will you trust your man, Sam Keller?"

"Without a doubt."

"He is three rooftops in that direction," Kil'Sin'Deres said, "If you would go speak to him, he will vouch for what I would ask of you."

"I'll be right back," he said, "Bel, keep an eye on him."

"Yes, Prophet."

Rictor was gone for about ten minutes before he returned to the rooftop with a grin.

"OK, what is it ya need?"

"I have a plan to help Rash'Tor'Ri with the hordes of Kresh on his world. I require a number of your Human Soulguard to leave the right impression behind."

"A plan to help him? By all means, share that," Rictor Hughes said with a vicious smile.

***

I awoke from a deep sleep with a gasp.

"Holy shit!" I said as I jumped from the bed.

"What is it?" Lyrica asked as she came from the bed with fire beginning to roll across her naked body.

"That's just sexy," I said, "but it's not that sort of Holy shit."

She looked at me with that look, "It better be important."

"I feel them," I said, "I feel them all."

"Who?"

"The Kresh," I said, "Kil'Sin'Deres must have done something on the other side."

"That's good news," she said.

"Yeah," I said, "but now we have to get everyone to stop shootin' at 'em long enough to get 'em off planet."

"Hmmm."

"Exactly."

www.ingramcontent.com/pod-product-compliance
Lightning Source LLC
Chambersburg PA
CBHW031943130726
47905CB00002BA/489